Small World

By

Katina Rosser

Small World by Katina Rosser

Published by My Block Publishing LLC

Copyright © 2021 Katina Rosser

katinarosser.com

katinarosser@gmail.com

Disclaimer: The characters in this book are all fictional. Any resemblance to actual person(s) dead or alive is entirely coincidental.

ISBN: 978-0-578-95228-4 Print

I dedicate this book to my hometown, Lagrange Georgia. As the saying goes, *"You come here on vacation and leave on probation."* It wouldn't be right if I didn't give my readers a glimpse into the Trap.

Table of Contents

Chapter One: Kim

While I sat waiting for the financial aid advisor to return from the printer, I noticed the lack of windows in her office. How one could sit in an office for eight hours a day without sunlight was beyond me. Besides, I never wanted to be in a place where I couldn't see who or what was coming. I was beginning to get claustrophobic just sitting there thinking about it. The office door opened. My advisor handed me the forms that I needed.

"Thank you, Mrs. Jones. I'm really looking forward to starting class in the Fall," I said as I started to fill out the forms.

"You're welcome, Miss Davison. Your new future begins here, and I wish you much success," she replied.

Mrs. Jones was the last person I had to see before being officially enrolled in the Accounting program at Atlanta Technical College. After her long lecture about why I should not take out any student loans, went in one ear and out the other, I signed the subsidized, unsubsidized loan agreements and the PELL Grant application and walked out of the office. After tuition and supplies, the student loan stipends would come far in between, but every little bit helped. Getting money was on my mind at all times, especially today since my utilities were turned off while I was getting ready to leave to enroll in school. Although it wasn't by any fault of mine, I had to put it on my to-do list today, which interfered with my hustling. There was nothing to do but laugh when it happened. Shit happens when you don't handle your own business and rely on others to do the right thing; they usually don't. I've found that no matter how much you help people, they still have the potential to fuck you over. So, I kept my eye on everything and everybody. At least I tried to.

I'm not a whiny type either. You wouldn't find me crying and being emotional over little dumb shit. I took my bitterness with my sweet and kept things moving. However, today's mishap confirmed that I needed a positive change in my life. The sooner, the better because my latest male sponsor, Peter, had, had enough of my shit and decided to put his position up for bidding.

Peter was a corporate lawyer, I'd been seeing. He wanted to get married, and I didn't, so I had to pull a ninja move. Get to the money quickly and get out. Poor Peter hung in as long as he could, but he caught on to the game that I was running. He desperately needed commitment on the table for the money he was putting out, but I wasn't going to give it. It was just a matter of time before things ended. When he asked where the relationship was going, I could tell that he wanted real love, but that was something I just couldn't give to someone like him. Not now or ever. So, I replied with the usual "It's not you, it's me." He was crushed. We ended the relationship, and with that went a two grand per week allowance, a lavish loft in downtown Atlanta, a GLE63 Mercedes-Benz, endless shopping, and luxury getaways. But hey, easy come, easy go.

I'm glad I wasn't dumb enough to give up my house on the south side. I'd been letting an old friend, Tanya, stay there while I was off living my best life. She needed a place to stay after her parents had disowned her for the millionth time, so she asked to stay in my crib. She had become a live-in nanny to my kids and general house manager. However, she hadn't paid the utilities this month because she forgot due to the stress of going to her father's funeral. I've noticed Tanya has been overlooking a lot lately. She had been dealing with an addiction to crack cocaine and prescription pills for years. Despite her vices, she was one of my best friends. She'd been around through thick and thin, and I trusted her with my life. Which is why I made it my business to take care of her.

However, I only let her know what she needed to know because she talked so damn much. She would talk to anybody anywhere, and I don't like anyone in my business.

Tanya doesn't know how much money I am getting. I gave her money to pay bills to feel like she was responsible and productive and not all lost in her drug habit. I just didn't know the utilities would be cut off this quickly, or I would've made time to pay it myself. It's definitely not a problem, though, because I managed to save up forty grand in six months. I knew one day Peter was going to wake up and bounce. His kind always did. Men with money and power always thought that they could buy love, but they always ended up with their pockets emptied and unhappy fooling around with me. Sorry about your luck Peter Norton. Your services are no longer needed.

My love has never been for sale. Hell, I've been rocking high-end shit since high school, so a nigga couldn't impress me with material shit or good sex. A nigga had to bring more than a checkbook and good dick to make me straighten up and fly right. I wanted a man to make an effort to fuck my brain. I liked intellectual hood guys. Men who are intelligent, family oriented, money-driven, and have CEO potential, yet their persona seemed one-sided to the naked eye. You have to peel their layers very carefully, but these types of men are rare. You won't find them standing on street corners making flashy loud plays to impress his homeboys. They were usually in secluded upscale places, trying to plot on getting out of the illegal game they're in. Although I don't consider myself a hood chick, I'm far from stupid, and a nigga had to be able to maneuver in the same silent fashion as I did. If he can't be a chameleon, he would never hold my attention.

Peter was a straight-up and narrow guy with nothing but business sense. He couldn't see past himself to recognize the game until it was too late. He thought that the world revolved around him and that he knew how to fix everybody's life. Once I saw he was an easy target, trust me, I didn't hold back. I sold him on the "innocent country girl" routine by telling him I had big dreams but wouldn't have any idea how to accomplish them without a strong, smart man like him in my life. I had to laugh at myself sometimes because I bet, he was somewhere calculating how much money he spent to end up with nothing. Oh well. I hope he will find someone that will treat him right. It just wouldn't be me. It was time for me to regroup and figure out my next move or who the next victim would be. There was money to get, so I didn't have time to waste sorting out people's feelings. We all get the same twenty-four hours in a day. I can't worry about what someone else did with theirs. Like I said, ninja money moves.

The only legal income I had coming in was from C&M's Tax Services, a small Mom-and-Pop tax company. However, I hadn't been to work in two weeks because I had to run around town, getting old high school transcripts and paperwork to start school. The job wasn't stable because it consisted primarily of seasonal tax preparations.

However, it was okay for me because it was flexible enough for me to maneuver. I met the owners, Clyde and Mary Dawson, at a coffee shop when I first moved to Atlanta ten years ago. They saw something in me that I didn't see myself. Potential. Somehow, they thought I'd be a successful businesswoman one day. They managed to take me under their wing, and in return, I was the daughter they never had. Clyde and Mary are the embodiment of black love. We recently celebrated their 50th anniversary. They had two sons, one biological and one adopted, that they don't say much about. They also had a nice financial cushion set up for their retirement. I looked up to them. They were my role models and couple goals. I would do anything for them, including enrolling in college, per their request.

As I walked out of the Financial Aid office, I knew Mrs. Jones' snobby ass thought she had sized me up, I guess from how I was dressed. But she just didn't know, I may look like a well-to- do conservative, but I'm as grimy as grimy could get. However, I looked like a million bucks today, but it isn't from what that heifer was thinking. Just like men in power, most women in authoritative positions size other women up by their attire, school, or sorority affiliation. Today, my intention was to impress with my attire. Everything I had on from head to toe was HOT, courtesy of Peter. What Peter didn't know didn't hurt him. I saved the forty grand by telling Peter that I was shopping with the allowance money. However, I copped all the clothes, shoes, and purses with stolen credit cards. He never asked for receipts. All he wanted was for me to look good when we went out, so I made sure I did. It wasn't nothing because my long slender-curvy body made anything look good.

The high-end store clerk never thought twice about the fake IDs and stolen credit cards, courtesy of my African friend Kawame. When I placed today's black Armani suit on the counter at Neiman's, the salesclerk just smiled a quirky grin. I guess she was thinking about the commission she was going to make, or maybe she was looking at the CELINE bag I was toting. All I knew was, the suit would make me look like I was about business, and that's the look I was going for today. I politely took my signed loan copies and left. Mission accomplished.

Mrs. Jones thought I was enrolling in school to get a great education and to advance my career. In reality, I was going back to school to make the Dawson's happy and get the money from financial aid. Free money was always a plus in my book. The Dawson's suggested that I get an accounting degree. They wanted me to learn the new tech savvy ways of tax preparing and take their company to the next level. I could care less about the education because I know a career is almost impossible in this new, unforgiving workforce for felons. I caught a felony theft case twelve years ago, and lord knows I'm still explaining it to this day. Society was right about one thing: once you go down that hustling path, it's hard to reroute your hunger for fast money to a legit career.

I guess that's why I'd always been more attracted to street niggas. I didn't judge anyone who was trying to survive the cards they had been dealt. When Obama was the president, companies had gotten firmer on not hiring convicted felons and blacks. Hell, people who didn't have a criminal history couldn't even find a job, which left me at the bottom of any hiring list. I didn't sweat it though; I just made it do what it do. I supported myself and my kids by any means necessary. When life throws you lemons, my motto was that you fry fucking lemon pepper wings and chill out until the next opportunity presents itself. As the rappers preach, it's a million ways to get paid. If you have common sense, street sense, and book sense, you can maneuver around all the loopholes the corrupt United States has to offer.

I sat through Mrs. Jones's speech with my eyes open, listening for the part when she told me how much money I would personally be getting from the student loans. Every eight weeks, I would be getting $7500. I've always been good at math. Before she could complete her calculations on the calculator, I blurted out the correct amount. She looked at me with confidence. However, this amount and going to work at least three days a week, would give me an income of about six grand per month. Plus, whoever my next victim was, wouldn't know I had financial aid, and he will have to come out -the- pocket for school payments that don't exist. I intended to use his contributions to pay on the student loans to shoot my credit score sky-high for future advancements. That monthly income didn't include my side credit card hustle with Kawame. Because it varied, I used it for my play money, and I played hard. In Hood Finance 101, I learned to have multiple cash money incomes. That way, losing one didn't affect my livelihood. I've always lived by the win-win concept. Losing Peter didn't stop one damn thing in my world.

I must say, Kawame kept my operation tight for a few years. His African crew was the bomb with hacking credit card accounts. They even had a guy who made IDs to match the name on the credit card. Not to mention a chick who works in the credit card fraud department who manages the card activity. She lets us know when to ditch the cards and IDs. We get high-end stuff to sell but keep what we want for ourselves. With this setup, I will still have days available to see my Lil boo, Jaylen, about twice a month.

Jaylen was a small-time drug dealer I met through a mutual friend. I didn't really like him like that, but being with him was a guaranteed fifteen hundred dollars each visit. Sometimes more, depending on how well he was doing in the streets. I could quickly clear about fifteen grand per month, undocumented and undetected by my DFCS counselor. They couldn't lower or terminate my government benefits if my income from the tax company said that I was struggling. There you have it, hood rich life in a nutshell. It's not as easy as it looks on TV, but hey, somebody had to do it. Why not me? A bitch had to always stay on her shit to live the life I lived. Some people judged; some loved it, and some hated it. However, I didn't give a hill of beans about either one. I was doing what I do to survive, and it worked for me. I'm happy. My kids are happy. That's all that mattered to me.

When I left Mrs. Jones, I nearly sprinted to the parking lot. But someone caught my eye and slowed my pace. I always observed my surroundings no matter where I was. I noticed a guy sitting at the bus stop near the campus. He was looking good and rocking the latest Philipp Plein gear. He had to be from up North because niggas from Georgia didn't know anything about the Philip Plein clothing line. To get a closer look, I made it my business to ride past him. Damn, I was glad I didn't sell my car like Peter had suggested. He wanted to sell it and let me continue to drive his Benz. But one thing I learned about lame guys, was that you could have anything they had as long as you're with them. As soon as the relationship goes left, so did their contributions. For that reason, I always tried to keep my own money. When it was time to leave, I could jet with no problem. Fortunately, this ML550 I owned was okay for what I had going on. If I had sold my car, I would be at this damn bus stop sitting beside this nigga instead of cruising by.

I wanted to get a closer look to see what shoes "bus stop cutie" had paired with his ensemble, so I put on my glasses to get a better view. I was always looking for people to sell stuff to. To my surprise, he and I made eye contact, something I tried to avoid. The less eye contact you share with a person, the less chances of having feelings for them when it is time to take their money. I blew the horn to say hello, but he flagged me down. I pulled over and rolled down the window. His Bond No. 9 Scent of Peace cologne made me want to seduce his fine ass right there, but I didn't have time to play today. I was in my "college girl professional" mode. Plus, I didn't need a bus stop stalker hanging around campus looking for me if I didn't answer or return his calls.

He leaned into my car with a big smile on his face. I noticed his teeth were white and straight. They were almost perfect. His mouth moved.

"Hello, beautiful. Can I get a ride?"

The thought of a nigga approaching me with this lame ass shit made my face frown. I almost drove off, but something about him was intriguing, so I kept my foot on the brakes and put the car in Park.

"You should have a ride coming every fifteen minutes. Correct? You are standing at a bus stop." I laughed. He smirked.

"Can I take you to lunch, beautiful," He asked.

"Why would I do that and were you on your way to lunch before I pulled over?"

"Sort of, but I was waiting for you to come out of the school, so I could ask you to go with me." I gave him the "yeah right" look.

"Oh Okay. I get it. You are a psychic bus rider! How tempting." He laughed at my sarcasm.

He points to the campus diner across the street to suggest we go there. I can't lie, I was hungry as hell because I didn't have breakfast. So, I accepted the invitation. Lunch couldn't hurt. Plus, I haven't seen his shoes yet, and I really want to see them. I parked my car back in the parking lot and walked over to meet him at the diner. As I crossed the street, I laughed to myself because this suit and heels are not made for walking. I felt so silly strutting across the street, but then I saw him looking at me, from inside the diner. He had a smile on his face, but I couldn't read it. It could be that he was happy to be having lunch with me or he's just lusting for my ass. Whichever one it is, I'm about to find out.

I sat down in the booth. He leaned in and took my hand into his. He smiled as he said, "I need to know your name before we eat, or I'm goin' to think you just usin' me for a meal." I burst out laughing. I shook his hand sternly as if we were two businesspeople meeting at an office.

Playfully, I said, Forgive me sir. Hello. I'm Kim, and who do I have the pleasure of having lunch with today?"

He properly introduced himself as Keith Thomas and I responded, "Nice to meet you, Keith."

I'm terrible with names, and I probably wouldn't remember it, but I always asked anyway. I'm so glad he chose to sit near the window. I had a habit of sitting where I could see who was coming in and out of an establishment. I never wanted any of my old flings to catch me off guard and walk up on me in their feelings about some bullshit I had put them through.

I didn't give Keith my last name because I was more cautious about giving out personal information. Nowadays, people are quick to get your info and hack your life. This Facebook and Instagram shit got stalkers in full effect. Plus, in my line of hustle I see how people's information got taken through casual conversations.

"Do you attend this college too?" I asked.

"No, I was really waitin' on you to come out of the school. I saw you pull into the parking lot, and before I could get over to you, you darted into the office. You were walkin' fast as hell in those heels. But I must say you do it effortlessly," he complimented.

I proudly looked down at my thousand-dollar Gucci pumps and caught a quick glimpse at his alligator-skinned Maury sneakers. This nigga's dress game was on point from head to toe. *Why was he on the bus?* I bit more into the conversation to see if I could find out more.

"Boy, stop playing. You were not waiting on me to come out of the school. How would you know I would stop and talk to you?"

"I really wanted to meet you. I was going to wait by your car, but I thought that would look too stalkerish, so I sat at the bus stop and waited to see you come out," He replied.

I agreed, it was beginning to sound weird because here, my ass was sitting in a fucking restaurant with him. I needed to stop being so damn curious and impulsive. People were getting crazier by the minute. Especially, these niggas who can't accept rejection.

To my surprise, Keith's conversation was interesting enough to hold me up for two hours. He told me he was originally from Georgia. He just moved back to Atlanta from New York. His ATL tattoo and out-of-placed Philip Plein gear confirmed this. He told me he had a job interview earlier, which he didn't get because of his criminal background. I had to ask what he had been in prison for. Having kids, I couldn't associate myself with a damn child molester. He gave a vague answer of trafficking, which I already suspected. However, I'm always relieved when guys confirm that they were not out here checking for little girls or little boys, for that matter. I told him just enough of my business to keep him interested. He gave me his number without asking for mine which I appreciated. Most of the time, I really don't have any interest in talking to them ever again. I just liked to see what people are up to and if I could make some money with them in the future.

After lunch, Keith walked me to my car, and I pulled off with no intention of calling him unless I had a pair of size ten high-end shoes to sell. I liked that he left the ball in my court because I always liked to choose who I spent my personal time with. I was too busy hustling to be boo'd up. It has been a minute since I was in a real relationship. Truth be told, I'd only had one genuine relationship in my thirty years, and it ended in divorce. Therefore, I'm not trying to start up with anyone new. Since my divorce, I had lived a very carefree life, and drama was not in my vocabulary. My ex-husband, Marcus, was the lamest nigga I ever met, but he promised me a nice drama-free life. Boy, did he deliver!

Being married to him was the most boring time of my life. I was so miserable.

When I met Marcus, I had just moved to Atlanta from Newnan, Georgia with two young daughters. He promised me a simple life to raise my kids in. I had moved from the small town looking for better opportunities for my children and a big city playground for me. I ended up falling for his bullshit and we got married within a few months of meeting. It was good until it wasn't. We were from two different upbringings, and we collided a lot. He had come from a two- parent household and I was the product of a single mother. He was from the city, and I was from what some call the country. If you didn't know us, you would think we had grown up in opposite lifestyles because I had more street smarts than Marcus. Newnan is small but ain't nothing slow about it. Everybody knew everybody, which made it harder for me to prosper. To make it even harder, everybody knew my family. My dad was a low-life pimp who loved money over everything. He was very abusive to women, and everybody knew him to be a womanizing dog.

One night my dad beat one of his white prostitutes so severely; she was in a coma for a week. It turns out she was an underage runaway, and her family was outraged when they found out what my dad had done to her. Her father was a well-connected, overzealous police officer who terrorized our small black community for years. Officer

Antonio Brown was relentless in the early '90s, and he wasn't going to stand for a black man pimping his daughter. A few days later, my father was hauled off in an unmarked car. He was missing for weeks.

Then one night, my mom pulled my older brother and me out of bed at 3:00am and took us down with her to the city morgue to identify my dad's mangled body. She had witnessed this man beat women regularly when his money was short. She had taken many blows to the face herself over the years, so when she saw him lying there lifeless, she shouted, "Good riddance, you dirty bastard." I remembered hearing my brother's heart skip a beat as I lay on his chest. He ran with me in his arms to my mom's side. She never shed one tear. I remembered looking at all the resentment in her face. I looked down at my father, and his eyes were gouged out with his tongue cut from his mouth. I noticed a torn fifty-dollar bill still tightly gripped in his hand. Even in death, he held onto the money. On the ride home, the radio was playing, and I remember my mom singing along with Patti Labelle's 'On My Own.' She seemed so content. I vowed that day at five years old to never let a man live if he ever put his hands on me or took money from me. I grew up putting money first, and my ability to feel emotions died with my dad.

My dad's ways branded my family though. I moved in silence in order to not bring additional attention to them, especially my mother. She had gone through so much. Our family never spoke of the incident, or at least I never heard anything about it from them. Maybe they thought I was too young to know, but who knows. My mom moved to a new neighborhood to get a fresh start. I learned later she got a reasonable insurance settlement from my father's death. Consequently, I had a peaceful childhood. After my father's death, my family moved on to a better life, but somehow everyone in the small town still knew our story.

Small town gossip was normal in Newnan, and it's usually only a third of the truth. So, I never wasted time giving gossip any energy. I buried the memory of my dad in the back of my mind, and I only retrieved it whenever a muthafucka chose to try me. The last memory of my dad was from his funeral. I was lying on my brother's shoulder, as I observed this out-of-place white woman sitting in the back of the church. Her face would forever be embedded in my mind. She was the girl who was responsible for my father's death. She was Tanya

Chapter Two: Two Peas in a Pod

Once I was old enough, I located Tanya. She's still in my life today. Since she was responsible for both of our lives going in the direction it took, I thought we should at least know each other. Despite who her dad was, she was actually a good person. I could see why my father had her around. It's always good to have a white girl on your team. She helped me, and I helped her. We were the dynamic team nobody saw coming. As a white girl, she could get in some doors I couldn't. She was a great asset to have because Lord knows, my temper could go from 0 to 100 in a split-second, so I tried to avoid conflicts, but some characters in this world have most certainly taken me there, and I showed them that there was some hood under all these designer clothes. If someone crossed me, the "get back" may come long after, but they best believe it was coming.

I had a heart of gold, though. For example, taking care of Tanya and my twins. I didn't birth my twins; they were the creation of my best friend Tashia, aka Truffle, who was killed in a drive-by shooting. She was eight months pregnant when some niggas shot her down on her mom's front porch. The twins' father, Calvin, was serving life for retaliating against one of Tashia's killers. The street's scenario was, Calvin's crew had robbed a nigga, and the guys' crew came back for blood, so Calvin had to go back just as hard. It was a miracle that the twins lived through the ordeal. Unfortunately, Tashia and her mom didn't, so I stepped in and vowed to take care of the kids until my death. When he can, Calvin sends me money from prison to help with the girls. Hell, he was making more money than some of these niggas out here on the streets. I admired his hustle and respected him a lot. The twins and I made the trip down south to Coffee County State Prison every Sunday. Calah, meaning *Opportunity,* and Takara, meaning *Treasure*, were my world. I made sure that they maintained a relationship with their dad because he was the only biological family member that they had left. Unfortunately, Calvin's mother was deceased, and he had no siblings. Tashia's brother died a few months after she did. He was self-medicating the loss of her and their mother and ended up overdosing on some painkillers. It was just too much for me, so I moved to Atlanta to get the twins out of the drama and introduce them to better opportunities. I never wanted them to go through that small town bullshit where people would whisper and judge them for what happened to their parents. I think we lived pretty well, considering where we came from.

After lunch, I pulled into my subdivision and smirked at the homes' value sign. Two hundred grand to five hundred grand. Shit was crazy because my wannabe high-class ass neighbors don't know how I bought my house. I paid for my home within ten years. Calvin and I gave the Dawson's a hundred grand down payment to put down on the house. I rented it from them on Section 8 for eighteen hundred dollars per month. The mortgage was only nine hundred. I had a goal to pay the house off in ten years, so I always paid thirty-six hundred dollars per month towards the mortgage. After the ninth year, the house was paid off. The Dawson's signed the deed over to me in year ten. I don't socialize with the neighbors but judging by the multiple foreclosure signs in the yards, I know their asses were struggling to pay their mortgages.

I used different government assistance programs to help pay the bills and keep my refrigerator stocked. I read the complaints about taxpayers footing the bill for us to live the way we do. To that, I say, fuck them! Don't hate me because I know how to work the system. I wasn't out here robbing or killing. I'm just trying to survive. Don't get me wrong, I understand why the Middle Class is upset. They are struggling living paycheck to paycheck, eating ramen noodles. All while people on food stamps are eating better than them. But being righteous has a price to pay, and if that's what you value, you get what you ask for. America was built on greed. So, fuck what you heard. I love to eat good, and I'm going to feed my family by any means necessary. Period.

I was raising my kids to be well-mannered, smart, and respectful. I made a way for them to go to the best schools. I gave Tanya the responsibility of registering the twins into private school. It's amazing how money talked within these institutions. No one ever questions a white woman enrolling her two high yellow nieces into the school, especially after telling them her sob story of how she wants to spend all her inheritance on getting her nieces an excellent education because it was their mother's dying wish. Hell, I was thankful for the system because it allowed me to give my kids opportunities, they would never have had based on a minimum wage income. You had to assimilate and act the part. Don't hate the player, hate the fucking game.

Despite my luxury lifestyle, I didn't trust too many people in my home or my life. I had to protect my girls and Tanya at all costs. If anyone ever got salty and wanted to hurt me, they wouldn't know where I lived or who to go after. I especially didn't let niggas come around the twins or Tanya. They tend to get relaxed when they find out about a chick having a good setup. They'll get good pussy, start eating good healthy food, spending more time in the fucking suburbs than the streets. Then, they want to lay back and daydream about giving up their hustling days and flying straight and narrow. But they failed to realize I hated the lame nine-to-five boring-ass niggas. Hell, the government programs, caseworkers, hustling, and raising children was a full-time job. The shit was a hustle in itself. So, the less men knew about my finances, the better. After my divorce from Marcus, I promised myself two things: One, that I'd never marry again. And two, that I'd never be broke, the way I was when I was married to his ass. If a nigga wanted to be with me, he had to know how to maneuver with me or get the fuck on. If we couldn't upgrade each other, then there was no need to be together. Like Sweet Brown says, "ain't nobody got time for that."

I walked into my darkened house. With the power off, the place felt dead. I took my wallet out of my purse, pulling my debit card out. I called Georgia Power to restore the service. Still, the representative told me that I'd have to come into the office. The bill was six hundred. I quickly changed my mind about paying it and decided to call Jaylen to pay it instead.

I had to call him before Georgia Power closed, but I had to prepare myself first. I rushed upstairs and took a shower. Thank God the gas was still on so I could have hot water. After moisturizing with cashmere oils and spraying on my Chanel Chance perfume, I slipped on a cute maxi dress with no panties or bra. Observing myself in the mirror, I looked too damn good to even be entertaining this nigga. Jaylen liked to get straight to business, and I don't have time for no mushy love making anyway, so the dress is for easy access. *Let's go get this paper.*

I dialed his number. Jaylen picked up with a familiar greeting. "What up, Shawty?" I asked where he was. He told me West End Mall. I don't know why I asked because he's always there or somewhere near there. He hardly ever left his comfort zone of the Westside. With my fingers crossed, I plead my case.

"I need to see you," I said in my best baby girl voice.

He always fell for that no matter how busy he was. For some reason, he loved to think that I missed his ass. I *hated* having sex with him, so I limited our sessions to twice a month or in case of emergencies. Today qualified as one, so I needed to put the pout down strongly. I need for him to say come right now because time is of the essence today.

"Daddy, I really miss you," I cooed.

He lowered his voice as if he were trying to avoid being heard by those around him.

"Oh, shit! Baby girl needs to cum for JRock? That's what's up."

I hated when he used his nickname. Everybody in the hood had a nickname or a shortened version of their real name. I bet it drove teachers crazy when they tried to teach kids their government name after the kid had been called Stank poo for the first six years of their life. I also detested when Jaylen obnoxiously talked in third person, but I didn't let on my frustration. I listened intently, hoping to hear what I needed to hear.

"Meet me at the crib. I should be there in twenty minutes," Jaylen instructed.

If he could've seen me pumping my fist in the air as if I'd just hit a Georgia Lottery scratch-off, he probably would've rescinded his offer.

"Cool. I'm on my way, baby."

I ended the call and ran downstairs. Getting a Sticky Note pad out of the kitchen drawer, I scribbled a note: *Order pizza. I'm out paying bills. The power may be out for a minute. They are working on the lines.* The less the twins knew about my adult life, the better. I attached forty dollars to the sticky note and laid it on the kitchen table. When the girls get home, they'll know what to do. Although my girls didn't know of my lifestyle, they had confidence that I would guide them in the right direction.

****

25

I waited for Jaylen in his driveway as I watched his uncle, Cliff, who was his live-in handyman, cut the grass. I waved and smiled. Turning the lawnmower off, he walked over to me and asked who I was looking for. He'd seen me a million times, but regardless he always requested. I told him Jaylen was meeting me and that he was on the way. I guess he had to clarify my presence just in case I was on some "pop up" type shit, trying to catch Jaylen with another chick or something. If only he knew, I couldn't care less who the nigga fucked with. A chick could get hers because I was damn sure going to get mine. Cliff turned around and walked back towards his mower.

Jaylen pulled in behind my car and hopped out of his G -Wagon. I got out and walked up to him, throwing my arms around his neck. Whispering in his ear, I said, "Hey, daddy."

He squeezed my ass and then patted it. Jaylen then whispered in my ear, "I can't wait to fuck the shit out of you." He threw up a deuce to his uncle and led me into the house while motioning his uncle the signal not to disturb us. I'm sure Cliff had been trained not to bother Jaylen unless it's money to be made or the cops showed up. Anything else could wait.

The nigga didn't even get the door shut before he simultaneously unzipped his Tru Religion Jeans and stepped out of his Jordans. I grabbed his hand and playfully pulled him to the bedroom. I needed to get this over with as quickly as possible. It was already 3:00 pm, and Georgia Power closed at 6:00pm. When we entered the room, I pulled the maxi dress over my head and laid back on his bed.

"Damn baby, you really missed daddy, huh?" Jaylen asked.

I gave him a seducing look as I opened my legs. He pulled out a magnum condom and threw it on the bed beside me as if to say: *you're about to get this big dick today, girl.* Within seconds, he was on top of me, proceeding with his ritual, hunching his deflated dick against my Brazilian waxed pussy.

He mumbled some dumb shit, "Who you been fuckin' Shawty? That nigga must not been doin' his job."

I moaned a little and lied. "I ain't been with nobody, boo. I've been waiting on you." He was instantly aroused.

He rose to his knees and opened the gold wrapper with his teeth. He struggled with the condom because his little dick ass couldn't fit a magnum. It killed the mood every time because, by the time he got it on, my mind was somewhere else. I think he got some sexual pleasure from me watching him do it, so I just let him. I closed my eyes and imagined that I was somewhere on a beach getting a massage from TI or somebody as equally damn fine.

I opened my eyes as Jaylen eased himself into my wetness. He started stroking, moaning like a seal. My lack of emotional and sexual feelings for Jaylen made me feel like a limp seal in heat, pressed against an iceberg. I just needed to play my role long enough to get the money. Some people may call my tactics gold-digging or whoring, but I called it surviving. I lay still while Jaylen rough fucked me for about twenty minutes before he finally came. He rolled off me with delight, grinning at me like a kid at Christmas.

He ran his fingers through my messy tresses and said, "Damn, daddy fucked up his baby hair today. Didn't he?"

I laughed and said, "Yeah, you always do. I think you do it on purpose, so I won't go anywhere but home."

"My girl needs to be at home and not hangin' in these streets. These wolves don't need to be houndin' my rare diamond," he said with authority in his voice.

He always tried to convince me he was the boss in the Atlanta drug world, so he stayed talking reckless. Jaylen claimed to be making a lot of money, but he always complained about paying his family's bills or feeding his whole crew on the block. Somehow, he repeatedly failed to mention that he was the biggest trick in Atlanta. He paid chicks off the rip because nobody was checking for his ass any other way. I'd heard of Jaylen's name in hair salon gossip before I met him. A lot of chicks around Atlanta knew he was a paymaster. Still, I'm probably the only one that tried to make him feel better about it because I boosted his ego for the hell of it. It's actually funny because he was too dumb and arrogant to realize that people were just using him. But his money was good, so it was all good on my end.

I officially met Jaylen at my home girl's birthday party about a year ago. I noticed that he was spending major cash, but I wasn't searching for a man or a sponsor at the time, so I didn't really pay him any attention. I only went to the party because Daisy was the only female I dealt with, and she knew how to throw the best parties. I never made eye contact with Jaylen or spoke to him. But all the other girls at the party were all over his ass. I'd never been the thirsty type, so I never threw myself at a man. I didn't give a fuck if he had Bill Gates money. So, when Daisy called me the next day and told me Jaylen had asked her husband to get my number, I thought she misunderstood Jaylen's request. I figured he'd gotten me mixed up with one of the other girls there. She explained that Jaylen didn't like any of the girls because they were seeking too much attention. He wanted to meet me after watching me all night.

Daisy and I laughed because we both knew that nobody really knew the *real* me, not even her. She told me he was getting money on the streets, and her husband was always telling her about how the dude took good care of his women. *Ding, Ding, Ding!* That was music to my ears. I told her to text me his number. To be honest, I hated when people were in my business before we even started kicking it. He should've been man enough to approach me himself, but after our first date, I figured out why he didn't. He didn't know how to talk to women, and his ego was too fragile to allow himself to be turned down by one publicly.

The Jaylen I'd come to know was very insecure, and if he wasn't a street nigga, he wouldn't have gotten any play from women. His money was his only asset. It's sad because he wasn't a bad looking guy. He dressed well, drove a nice whip, and had a nice crib. He just didn't have any ambition to get out of the game. So, he was stuck trying to fit in, generation after generation, in the streets. That was neither here nor there because it was confirmed that Jaylen was a straight trick after our first date. He knew he had to pay a bitch to be with his simple-minded ass. His sex game was awful too. But Jaylen paid well, and that's what keeps women on his line. After our session today, I know I'm leaving with eighteen hundred dollars or more. Not bad for less than an hour's worth of work.

As we lay in bed, Jaylen started babbling about his street life, how he was the man, and how everybody was trying to hate on him. I didn't have time to listen to his petty little boy conversation, so I interrupted him mid-sentence. He was saying something about how he just posted a bond for one of his partners in New York. Lying, I told him I needed money for my mortgage. Back in the day, chicks played the "I'm pregnant" trick to get a few hundred out of a guy for an abortion. I learned that shit didn't fly too far with street niggas because their asses didn't mind having a bunch of children. I really didn't like having to go through all that, so I kept it simple. Give a nigga a sad story and ask for what you need. It always works. If he had it and wanted to continue fucking with you, he would give it up. If not, then he knew he had to step aside and let someone else get at you.

I sat up, grabbed my clothes, and went to freshen up in the bathroom. I always gave Jaylen a minute alone to get his money out of his stash. I'm not the robbing type of chick, so I had no desire to know where his hidden stash was. When I walked back into the room, he was fully dressed. He gave me a bear hug from behind, sticking the wad of money in my cleavage.

We walked out to our cars. He backed out of the driveway, giving me space to pull out ahead of him. Before I made the turn down the street, my phone vibrated between my legs. I looked down at the text from Jaylen.

Don't eva cum out da fuckin crib wit no bra & pannies AGAIN!!! Take ur ass Str8 home. I'll call you lata...LOL

. I burst out laughing, but I knew he was dead ass serious. I replied, *okay, Bae,* and pressed send. I made a left at the stop sign while Jaylen made a right. When he was out of sight, I pulled over and counted the money. I loved when a plan came together perfectly.

***

I pulled into Georgia Power's drive-thru at 5:30 pm. I strummed my fingertips on the steering wheel and huffed as I waited among the three cars ahead of me. When I got to the window, the customer service associate told me that I'd have to come inside to do *Reconnect* transactions. I zoomed around to the front and parked. The same bitch at the drive-thru walked to the counter to take my money with a stinking-ass attitude. I guess I had *hoe* written across my face because I wasn't wearing a bra or panties. Whatever it was, this bitch was rubbing me the wrong way. I hated dumb bitches with these little eight dollar an hour jobs acting like they were better than everybody because they had a job. I stared at her with disgust. I wanted to tell her, dumb-*dumb, I just made what you make every two weeks in one hour.* I looked at her thrift store outfit and worn-down shoes as she completed the transaction. I observed her name tag that read *Michelle.* Michelle asked if I was sure I wanted to put it all on the bill. I nodded, yes. I paid nine hundred dollars so that I wouldn't have to worry about paying the bill next month. Michelle gave me the receipt and said the power would be back on before 8:00 pm.

I laid twenty-five dollars on the counter and said, "Thank you, sweetie. Your smile and customer service were awesome today. Have lunch on me tomorrow." Michelle's mouth dropped as I walked out the door. I tried to spread love whenever possible because free money always comes and goes. I called it paying taxes. I figured if I gave a little away here and there, it would cut down on the losses.

I stopped at *Q-Time* drive-thru in the West End and ordered a veggie plate. I had let enough people see me without a bra and panties, so I dared not go inside. I disliked driving and eating, so I parked my car and ate. Plus, I needed to take a moment to reflect on my next move. Although today worked out just as I planned, there was always a new problem lurking. As I rolled down my passenger window for some fresh air, Keith came to mind. His fingerprints remained on the window, where he leaned on my car earlier. Damn, people be slipping. If I was a cop or private detective, he would've given his fingerprints without knowing it. I searched for his number in my contacts and called him. His voice was sexier on the phone than in person. That was strange, considering it was usually the opposite.

He answered with, "What took you so long to call me?"

I laughed. "I didn't know I had a time frame. Do you even know who this is?"

"Of course. It's Kim. You're the only person I don't have a contact name saved for. So, when are we goin' on our second date?"

I'm surprised he remembered my name. *Nice save, nigga, but I'm not falling for it.* "I must've missed the first date," I replied.

"You must've forgotten that I sat at that bus stop for an hour and a half waitin' to ask you out to lunch."

"Oh, that's what you call a date? I thought you just liked eating with strangers. My bad."

He shot back, "Well, I have to eat dinner later and breakfast in the morning. Which one are you up for?"

I realized he wasn't letting up, so I tried to redirect the conversation. "You sound like a pimp to me. Is that a side hustle you got goin' on?"

"How does a pimp sound because I surely wouldn't know. I'm just asking a lovely lady out for a meal like gentlemen should."

"Well, since you put it like that, I guess I don't have a choice. I'll have to say breakfast because I'm eating dinner right now," I said. I anticipated that he'd say something cliche like *your place or mine?* But to my surprise, he didn't.

"Can you meet me at the Dwarf House on Highway 85 in Riverdale, say about 9 am?"

I don't know why, but I agreed before hanging up. *This nigga be moving around on that damn bus. The Chick-fil-a he suggested was a long way from the school.* His outer exterior was giving me typical bum nigga vibes, but his conversation was giving me butterflies. I wanted to know more about him.

As soon as I walked into the house, Jaylen called to make sure I was home. I told him I had just gotten out of the shower and needed to rest for the night. He was cool with that. After I straightened up the house and the twins were in bed, I intended to do just that. I was grateful the lights were back on so the girls could enjoy their pizza and TV time. I chatted with them about their school day before cleaning up the empty pizza boxes on the coffee table and headed upstairs for a long hot shower. After getting the girls settled in for the night, I crawled into my king-size bed and checked my text messages.

TANYA: So sorry, Kimmie, I forgot to go pay utilities. They may cut them off.

ME: It's cool. I paid it. Just keep that money. I'm praying for you and your family.

TANYA: You sure?

ME: Yes. See you when you get back. <3

Although I felt no empathy for her father's death, I wanted Tanya to know that it was okay to feel sad about her father's passing. I know all too well how to love and hate a parent at the same time. I guess that's why she and I are two peas in a pod.

I lay my phone on my nightstand and closed my eyes. I wondered what I was going to wear to this little breakfast date with Keith in the morning. Whatever it was, I knew it was going to be cute.

Chapter Three: Keith

Today is going to be a good day. My nigga JRock, called me to see if I had any units left. He needed ten to sell to some country boys from South Carolina. I told him I only had two left but that I could get a hold of ten dummies if he wanted to get down like that with them niggas.

"Shiid, you can always flex them country boys. The shit is good, my nigga. It looks and registers like the real thing. You shouldn't have any problems gettin' paid with it," I said.

I was offering JRock a lick he couldn't afford to turn down. He replied, "Damn nigga, you got off yo shit quick. Who you gettin' that shit off on that quick? But you right, I don't owe these niggas no loyalty. Fuck it. It's a go."

I knew he would jump on this play because the JRock I knew was always lurking for a sweet lick. He is the Mad Max of our crew. You never knew what you were going to get with him. He'd been a wild card since we were kids.

With all the niggas he had taken out of the game, I'm sure he had his own graveyard somewhere. However, when he was on his "A" game, there was no stopping him from getting to the money.

"K, man, I'm down. So, fuck them, country ass lames. Let's run it," he confirmed. Ten units at thirty thousand each was enough to make JRock cross out his own mother. God rest her soul.

"Cool. Let's run it then."

I only trusted a few people, so my circle was small. It was me, JRock and Trey. We'd been friends since we were knee-high and have been running in these streets since middle school. After JRock gave me the green light, the play was in motion. It was on. I explained everything to Jay, and I told him to get with Trey and explain the move to him. Trey and I switched out playing the part of the main plug. He's up today and I'm playing the right-hand man that accompanied him to every transaction.

"Make sure you tell that nigga to pull up in the 750 and to wear his ice to make this shit look real. We don't need these fools doubting the movement," I instructed.

"Bet. I gotcha, my nigga," Jay answered.

Although JRock often forgot details, I felt confident that he and Trey would come through correct, because they were my boys. They'd never gone left field on any money play we'd done. I trusted them more than I trusted myself sometimes.

Trey was the super flashy nigga in our crew; he spent all of his money on clothes, jewelry, and fresh whips. I must admit, his BMW was the hottest thing on Atlanta's streets. He could afford it because we were moving a few units a week, and we split all the profits equally.

After I showered and put on my Philip Plein gear, I called my homeboy, Ace, to put the order in. Ace was the Dummy Brick King of Atlanta. He was the only nigga I knew who kept thirty or forty dummies on standby. His motto was to never keep your victims waiting. I dialed Ace's number and waited for him to answer.

"What's up, fool?" he greeted.

"I need what you got, homie. Let me hold ten of them things," I asked.

He quickly replied, "You know if you pull off the move, I need 10 bands, playa."

"I gotcha Bruh. Say less. I'm on the way to you right now," I confirmed.

"Bet," we say in unison before ending our conversation.

I drove my Dodge Ram truck because it was more lowkey than my other whips. I'm cocky as hell when I need to be, but I don't like unnecessary attention when I'm handling street shit. I just wanted to get to the money, save it and promote my music career. I'm too playa for that "Hot Boy" shit. I'm trying to transition into some Jay Z type shit. Hoping one day I'll find my Bey. Until then, I don't love these hoes.

I get to Ace's spot in less than an hour. As promised, he had the shit on deck. As we were loading the dummies into my trunk, I thought about how desperate I was to find an actual plug, because this flexing niggas shit ain't really what I be on. My last plug had caught a FED embezzlement case up in New York, so I had to get a new connection soon. They locked up about ten people when they came to scoop his ass up at his crib. Good thing we were just having dinner and no drugs were involved. They confiscated a few registered guns, but that didn't stop the cops from threatening to send every convicted felon to jail. It was illegal for convicts to be around a gun or anyone that had one. I sat upstate without bail or a fucking charge until they figured all that shit out. Fortunately, JRock and Trey drove there and picked me up because I had flown to New York. Although I don't mind leaving Atlanta to make moves, I loved being home. I have a home base advantage and I could predict these familiar streets.

As soon as I pulled off, I hit Trey up on his cell to tell him to meet me in our usual spot in Carver Homes

Projects. We all grew up there. They've recently been renovated. When white people started moving back into the city, the project look could not fit in. In other words, our hood got gentrified. They replaced our old stomping grounds with some modern apartments. They gave them a new name to disguise the frowned upon project activities. The shit didn't work because niggas were still getting money around the complex. It is just fewer niggas on the corners now. Plays are disguised with paperless transactions such as Cash App. Niggas ain't walking around with wads of money in their pockets anymore.

I give Trey the rundown on the part he was playing again in case JRock forgot to disclose any information. I always have to go back behind JRock because his ass was always playing under some chick, getting distracted and forgetting shit.

Trey and I met up and rode together to meet JRock at his spot. JRock's Trap house was near the highway, which is always convenient. Niggas who weren't from the ATL liked to have easy access in and out. We had to make these country boys feel comfortable enough to make this play. When we pulled up at Jay's spot, my phone vibrated. My little chick from Texas hit me up. The text read: *WHAT UP BOO?* Damn, she always hit me at the wrong time. I was constantly blowing her off, but business always came first. I texted back. *I'm busy. I'll hit you back later.* If I could pull this move off today, I would move to Texas with her.

My plan was to search for a plug out that way. Besides, a change of scenery was always good for a nigga like me. Especially after a play like today. The bonus was that she liked taking care of niggas, and she had access to a little bit of money. So, I knew I was good to get a few stacks from her to play with in Texas. She wanted to be down so bad, so that would make her feel like she was dealing with a broke nigga who needed her help. Women like that were oozing with the savior complex. They think they can get a nigga out of the streets with that petty ass money. Only a broke nigga wants to be taken care of by a bitch who can barely take care of herself. Only time I am up under a hoe like that is when I need a hideout.

After flexing some niggas, you never knew how a nigga was really rolling. You never wanted to be a sitting duck, so I'd lay low for a while with her until things calmed down here. These country niggas know where JRock spot was at, but he would be in the clear because the plan put him in a victim role. All he had to do was act like me, and Trey flexed him too, and he couldn't believe he'd been had. He would even play along like he was helping the niggas find us, but we would be long gone, and so would their damn money.

The three of us get in character and wait for the niggas to pull up. As the silver F150 pulled up, JRock, Trey, and I watched the two guys on the nigga rigged security monitor Jay had around the house. The windows are tinted but we could see through the front windshield, that the niggas were discussing something in the car, but we couldn't see who or what was in the backseat because the windows were tinted dark as hell. I saw the driver reach in the backseat and pull out a duffel bag. His mouth was moving, but I wasn't sure if he was talking to the dude in the front seat or someone in the back seat. I made a mental note of it in case some shit popped off during the transaction.

Two guys exited the car and walked to the door. JRock welcomed them in and escorted them to the kitchen table where Trey and I were posted with the dummies. We had the two real ones sitting up front, so it would pass any test that these country boys had up their sleeves. The taller one seemed nervous, and it was rubbing me the wrong way, but I kept my eye on him as I watched their car on the monitor. They couldn't see the monitor, so I could continue to watch without being noticed.

Trey made his sales pitch, "I hope y'all came to spend money on the best shit in Atlanta."

"Gee, I told your manz we about business. If you got it, we came to spend money," the guy holding the money bag spoke up.

He opened the duffle, and the cash was neatly stacked with hundreds and fifties. Trey offered him a seat at the table and instructed me to open the real key. The dude inspected the product, placing a little on his tongue. He sat back in the chair and gave JRock the nod.

JRock interjected and said, "I told you, my nigga, my people got that shit you want and need."

They high five, and the guy handed Trey the bag of money. JRock talked so fast and did his thing to distract the niggas, but he didn't even notice me strap up and get out of my seat. I saw the third nigga get out of the car and run to the side of the house. I shot that nigga in the head when he passed the window, and Trey quickly fired on the two standing in the kitchen. They fell to the floor right in front of JRock's feet.

Long story short, we had bodies and three hundred grand minus twenty grand. Ten for Ace and ten for my boy Calvin, who I was locked up with when I did time in Coffee County a while back. I owed that nigga a great deal for the knowledge and loyalty he showed me in prison. He saved my life up in there, and Trey and JRock understood that we had to give back to him on every lick we hit for keeping shit 100 while I was down. They never questioned it because they knew I would do the same for them to survive while locked up.

After snatching out a few teeth and removing any recognizable belongings on the dudes, we sat each of them up at the table as if they were smokers. We left pots cooking on the stove, a leaking can of gasoline sitting by the back door. One cigarette butt sent their asses up in smoke, or at least that's what the news reported the next day. Mrs. Carrie, the lady next door, confirmed that's what the police told her too. She held us down, so we held her down. She would now inherit that lot next door. We gave the young goons in the hood the South Carolina nigga's car and told them they could ride it for two days. Then instructed them to torch that bitch on a side street in Dekalb County somewhere.

Another day and another dollar in the safe. I stopped by the gas station to buy a new T-shirt. As I checked out at the register, Kim hit my line. I was shocked because I didn't think she would call, but I was glad she did. That let me know she was somewhat intrigued with me. I didn't know what made me stop to talk to her this morning, but it was something about her stride. I was at my PO office across from the school when I saw her walking into the college. She seemed confident and about her business. I liked all women, but I *loved* a woman that knew how to carry herself with ease. Most women thought they were cute or sexy, but few have true beauty. In reality, most niggas don't give a damn about what women wear. All we thought was how and when we are going to take it off. Now, if a woman holds my attention with her brain, she might be worth my time. But most females I had dealt with in the past were worried about the wrong things and they were dumb as hell. I couldn't roll with no dumb broad for long. If I did, she had something I needed of value, usually, a crib to lay low in or sex to get off, which was why I was headed to see Shawty in Texas in the morning as soon as I finished taking Kim to breakfast. I wanted to see more of what she was about. I told Kim to meet me at The Dwarf house at 9:00 am. Surprisingly, she agreed. I'm used to women playing hard to get, but Kim was different. She didn't hesitate. She seems confident in what she wants.

I dropped off the money at Ace, and we chopped it up for a minute. I didn't tell him what had happened earlier with the South Carolina boys. All he needed and wanted to know was that the deal was done, and the money was all there. Then I took my ass home to pack a bag for Texas. After a good shower, I lay in my bed, drifting off as soon as my head hit the pillow. In my drifting, I realized that I'd forgotten the Shawty from Texas' name. I have been calling her Shawty so much, I don't even remember her name. On another note, I reminded myself to ask Kim what her last name was when we met for breakfast tomorrow. I would have to find a discreet way to ask because I noticed that she hadn't given it to me, and I knew that was intentional. I noticed she got a lot of game.

Chapter Four: First Date

I woke up early to take care of some business. I had to sign the girls' permission slips for their field trip and email their teachers. I wanted to make sure that they were on track with grades and get a copy of the trip's itinerary and their chaperons' contact information. Managing twins can be confusing, but I've mastered it. Both were academically successful, which was a blessing because we were working toward getting them four-year college scholarships. That was another reason that I decided to go to college. I couldn't ask the girls to get their degree and not have one myself. I needed to lead by example. I didn't know what I would do once they left for school in a few years. They would be living in the dorm while I'd have the house to myself for the first time in my life. I know I will miss them terribly which is why I've decided to save my money to buy an Airbnb near their chosen college. Preferably a condo in the area closest to their university. Then they could move into the place after their freshman year if they wanted.

I waited until the girls left for school before I got ready for my breakfast date. I chose white INC black skinny jeans, a leopard-print short blazer and paired them with Gucci black patent leather loafers with a matching belt. I'm glad I chose not to wear a lot of makeup. Even in the morning, Georgia was too hot for all that shit on my face. In the summertime, I limited my makeup to eyeliner, mascara, and lip gloss. I pulled my hair up in a messy bun, slicked my baby hair down, threw on my Gucci shades, and made my way to the Dwarf house to meet Keith.

***

As I pulled into the Dwarf House parking lot, I was shocked at the number of cars lined up. It was so packed. Crowds made me nervous. I liked being in control of my surroundings. When there were too many people, things could get out of control. I called Keith to see if he was inside. He told me that he was pulling up. I got out of my car and walked towards the bus stop to meet him, but he cut me off in a black Buick Lacrosse. Wow. That's what I got for assuming. The nigga really wasn't riding the bus yesterday.

He rolled down the window and said, "Come ride with me."

"Damn, could a sister at least get a good morning or something? I thought we were eating breakfast?"

"We are. Just come ride with me somewhere," Keith insisted.

I hesitated for a second before I decided to hop into the passenger seat. We rode 85-North until we reached Hartsfield-Jackson Atlanta Airport. Keith parked in the hourly parking deck, got out, and opened my door. I had a habit of waiting to see if a nigga had home training. I sat and watched him walk around to my door. He definitely got a few brownie points for chivalry. I got out, and we walked inside the door that read N3. While walking through the atrium, Keith picked up a Creative Loafer from the newsstand. I looked at him like he was crazy because nobody really reads newspapers anymore. It's all digital now and can be downloaded. I chose to stay quiet because it was giving intellectual vibes. We entered Paschal's restaurant and sat in a cozy little corner. To break the ice, I asked, "Do you know something I don't know about the Dwarf House's food? We both laugh in unison.

"Nah. I just don't like crowds in small places. It was too crowded there this morning. I wanted a more secluded place, so we can talk", He replied with a big grin.

"Good, because I don't like crowds either. I'm glad you chose somewhere more private."

I loved Paschal's. I never noticed it was in the airport. Probably because it's nestled in a cozy dimmed lit corner on Concourse C. The soft jazz music gives it a romantic vibe. Eating in the airport always made me feel like I was going somewhere exotic. At that moment, I wished I was on a beach having breakfast with my attractive date.

The waitress took our order and promised to come right back with our expressos.

"Did you sleep well, beautiful?" Keith asked.

"I actually did. Did you?"

He tried to maintain a straight face as he told me that he was up all night thinking about me. I took that with a grain of salt. Niggas tried to convince the woman that they were their main priority, but only as long as she sat in front of him. I didn't listen to that bullshit. I redirected the conversation.

"What do you do for a living besides sell drugs," I asked.

He looked at me with disgust. "Why do you think I sell drugs," he said with displeasure.

"You told me you went to prison for trafficking. Remember? One thing I know is that prison doesn't have a track record of reforming people, so I just assumed."

"I also told you that I had just left a job interview. You just concentrated on the bad," he said with authority. He shook his head, disappointed.

"No, I'm sorry. I shouldn't have assumed that you were still in the game. So, what do you do, Mr. Thomas?" I asked again in a more intriguing way.

Selling drugs wasn't necessarily a vice, depends on who you ask. I wasn't a cop, nor did I judge anyone. As I said his name, I thought about how I should've googled him before agreeing to meet him again. I usually looked up people on the Department of Correctional information web page once they've told me that they've been in jail because niggas will tell you anything. I had to make sure that a nigga wasn't a child molester, woman beater, rapist, or any foul shit like that. He interrupted my thoughts.

"What do you do, Miss Kim?" he switched the conversation.

"I'm a Tax Preparer, and as of yesterday, I'm a full-time college student."

That was the only personal information that he was getting. At least it was the truth, even if it wasn't the whole story. I changed the subject to something less personal by asking who did his tats. They were so clear and unique. I could see the storyline in the detailed artwork. He told me that he got them while he was in jail. I wasn't surprised. There were some really talented tattoo artists in prison. Although I could only see his arms, I wondered if there were any more. I hated when a man undressed, and I got stupid shit like a nipple ring or tats of an ex-girlfriend's name on him. It pissed me off. My ex-husband had a nipple ring, and I hated it. Whenever we had sex, he always asked me to lick it. It made him cum faster, so I did it, but that shit seems suspect to me. To each their own, but I just didn't like those kinds of surprises. All niggas had flaws or some type of weird trait underneath their outer appearance. But I wish they would let a bitch know because some shit needed a warning.

Keith and I chatted for hours about life. He was easy to talk to. Not like some street niggas, with all that Shawty this and miss lady that. That was obnoxious and unnecessary. Keith's conversation had substance. We talked about politics, world business, and dreams. He loved reading the business section of the paper and the Creative Loafer helped him find the great restaurants in Atlanta that white people didn't want us to know about. He had a twelve-year-old daughter, Ariel, and his mom, Diane, who both lived in Florida. Like me, his father also died when he was young, but unlike me, his father was a cool dude who unfortunately succumbed to pancreatic cancer. Currently, music management and getting money were Keith's focus. Hell, money was all anybody should be focused on. The one thing that made our date awkward for me was that we had a lot in common. That was a first. We laughed at the same things. He was hood with an intelligent twist. I liked that. It was usually a hit or miss with me on a first date. But

I was feeling this nigga's swag, and he had my attention. I wanted to see where this would lead.

After breakfast, we walked around the airport. He asked me what I had to do today and if I was needed anywhere.

"Not really. My kids are on a field trip all weekend. Why what's up?"

"In that case, I hope you brought your ID with you."

"I did. Why?"

He walked up to the Delta counter and bought two one-way tickets to Texas. The service associate asked to see my ID, so she could print a ticket for me. After she finished the transaction, she handed us the tickets and said, "Thank you, Mr. Thomas and Miss Davison. Enjoy your trip."

We had two hours before take-off, and I asked about my car at the Dwarf House. Keith showed me a text on his phone. He texted a friend, Trey, with instructions for him to pick up my car on his tow truck and park it at his studio. Keith assured me that it would be safe there and that I could pick it up once we got back.

"I already took a picture of it, so he knows which one to get. "Don't worry, Kim. I got you covered. You're straight with me."

I sat up straight and looked him in the eyes and asked, "So you knew this was a go, huh?"

I wanted to read his facial expression, but he gave none. "No. But I'm glad it is, Miss Davison."

This nigga is good. I like how he got my government name on a first date. His finesse game is damn near as strong as mine. We boarded the plane and took our seats. Keith let me have the aisle seat, so I could stretch whenever I needed it.

"Welcome ladies and gentlemen to flight 278, Atlanta to Houston…" the captain announced before takeoff.

Chapter Five: Texas

I didn't plan on taking Kim with me to Texas, but I didn't want our date to be over. I was really feeling her and wanted to know more about her. I decided the easiest way to do this was to spend the weekend with Kim and then fly her back on Sunday. I desperately needed to stay in Texas to find a plug. It was weird that Kim was cool with coming on the trip, no questions asked. She didn't seem to be on hoe shit either. She may be used to niggas with money. I'd been a womanizer most of my life, so it was hard to trust a female. I watch everything they do. My mama taught me that women were the smoothest game runners on the planet, and that I should keep my eyes open, and my wallet closed. Unless I'm getting something of value in return, I don't give up my time too often. Pussy couldn't do it either. Every woman I'd ever met thought that their pussy was the best. They tried to sell that shit to the highest bidder or hold it back to get their way. But today, all I wanted from Kim was some conversation and her last name. I'd already gotten both. Anything else is a bonus.

We landed at *George Bush International* and caught an Uber to the first mall we came across. Kim insisted that she go shopping since she hadn't exactly planned for this trip and suggested we go our separate ways to shorten the amount of time in the mall. I agreed. She didn't ask for any money, so I hoped that she was straight. From afar, I saw her go into *Victoria's Secrets*, walking out with Bath & Body Works bags. I watched her go into a few other stores for outfits before making my way to Macy's to pick up Polo boxers and t-shirts. I also scooped up some Polo Blue cologne. It's not my usual scent but it will do. I hit up a store that sold Bally and Miskeen jeans. I copped a few outfits and met Kim at the food court. She was standing just where she said she would be. I'm glad she was on time because I'm not fond of waiting on a female, especially while shopping. Women took forever going in and out of stores. We grabbed some Chinese food and searched for hotels. We chose the Hilton because it was the closest distance to the stores and restaurants. I booked two rooms online since we agreed that it would be better to have separate rooms on this adventure.

Before we departed into our rooms, Kim handed me a bag with a toothbrush, toothpaste, men's body wash, and a wave brush. That's what I'm talking about. Because a brother had forgotten all that shit since our conversation had gone longer than I expected, and consequently, I'd left my damn bag for the trip. I had thought about walking to the *Walgreens* down the street to pick up some toiletries after settling in.

"Thank you, Miss Davison. You read my mind, huh?"

"You're welcome, Mr. Thomas. And, yes, I guess. What time are we meeting up later?"

"How about 7? I'll meet you in the lobby." "Cool!

See you then, Beautiful."

***

I didn't know how the fuck I ended up in Texas with this man, but damn, I needed this little getaway to try out this new American Express card and ID, Kawame gave me. It passed the initial test, so while Keith was doing whatever it was he had to do tomorrow, I'd be hitting the stores and the post office to send my loot back home.

I took a long hot shower. It was only 5 o'clock, so I had time to make some calls and check on the twins. They were having the time of their lives in New York with their debate team. I checked to see how Tanya was doing. I called intending to leave her a message, but she picked up on the first ring. She told me that her father had taken her out of his will. To make matters worse, her family didn't want her at the funeral. So, she was headed back to my house. I sometimes felt sorry for Tanya. She didn't deserve all the mistreatment from her family. Hell, my dad was a handful to deal with or resist. In fact, she was defeated from the moment she hooked up with him. She was searching for love in the wrong place, and it ruined her life. She'd been paying for it every day since. I told her she had the house to herself, and I would be back Sunday or Monday morning. I had no intention of staying any longer than that. I couldn't miss out on too much money fucking around with this dude.

Before Tanya hung up, she said, "Kimmie, I want to thank you for everything. I love you like a daughter. I have something important to tell you when you get back."

With a sigh, I said, "Aww, I love you more. See you when I get back."

I called my homegirl, Daisy, to see what she was doing and to find out what her plans were for her upcoming birthday. It wasn't until November, but this girl needed at least three months to plan because she always went big. I accidentally mentioned that I was out in Houston.

"Bitch, who the fuck are you out there with? I know people in Texas. Is he sexy, and does he have a friend?" she teased.

"I have no idea what you mean, sis. I'm out here working," I giggled.

"Yeah, workin' on some good dick is what your ass need to be doing, because I'm ready for some more God kids and a big wedding too. But anyway, I really do have people out there. I might need a favor while you out there. My cousin was supposed to send me some hair she trying to sell out there. I'll send her the money, but can you pick it up? Or can she bring it by the hotel you staying at? I need it sooner than later," Daisy pleaded.

"Yeah, I'm only mobile by Uber or Lyft, so just tell her to leave it at the front desk at the Hilton downtown. I'm in room 1107. Bye girl, I'll see you when I get back."

After hanging up with Daisy, I got dressed to meet Keith. I chose a cute little black Michael Kors dress and black leather strap sandals to match. I flat ironed my hair and wore it in a bouncy long bob. I was glad that I had my bronzer in my purse because it had my skin glowing. As I walked out of the room, I saw Keith headed to the elevator. He had on a pair of fashionable black jeans and a black shirt to match, but the Bally's really set off his whole outfit. Despite his fire fit, I was more turned on by him being here early. He held the door for me, and we went to the lobby and walked to the restaurant across the street.

***

Keith and I sat at the bar and talked for hours. We managed to drink an entire bottle of wine with a couple of shots of Patron. Some guy came to meet Keith, and they went outside for a minute. He came back in and asked me if I was ready to go. I was wasted, but I was alert enough to keep my eyes open for any bull shit.

"Yes. Are you?"

"Yeah, let's head back over to the hotel. It looks like it's about to rain, and I don't want you to get wet." Keith realized that he'd put his foot in his mouth. "Oh dang, I'm so sorry that came out wrong. I just meant that I don't want you to get stuck over here without an umbrella."

"Yeah, I see where your mind is but don't even try it, playboy. This is not going to be that type of party. What are you and that dude running, some type of sex trafficking or something?"

"Girl, hell nawl. You drunk and talking crazy. I met the dude when I went to *Walgreens* to get some deodorant and lotion since you were bein' stingy with yours. I asked him about some weed. He was just bringing it back. Come on, let's go with your drunk self." Keith was howling with laughter at my slurring and wobbling.

When we made it back to the hotel, Keith made sure that I'd be suitable for the night. I assured him I was good. I had Tylenol and water to keep me through the night. He thanked me again for a great time and for coming with him. When I staggered to the door, he kissed me on my forehead and retired to his room.

***

The next morning, I woke up to room service, flowers with a massage gift certificate attached to the bouquet. I read the outside of the card: *From the gentlemen next door.* Opening the card, it read, *Have a great massage! I have to go handle some business. I should be back by 3.- Keith.* Thank you, Jesus. Time to hit these streets. I jumped in the shower, got dressed, and booked an Uber. I hit every high-end store and boutique that I could find, then googled the nearest post office and packed that shit up and shipped it to Atlanta. I made it back to the hotel at 2 pm. I hoped that the spa could fit me in. After a bit of begging and lying, I was in and out of my session by 2:45. I went back to the room and showered. As I got dressed, Keith rang my phone.

"Right on time," I said aloud.

"What you up to? You good?" he murmured.

"Hello to you too. Yeah, I'm good. Just got out of the shower. Where are you?" I asked.

"Cool. I'm in my room getting dressed. I'll meet you downstairs in 20 minutes."

After putting on my best fit, I went downstairs to see Keith standing in the lobby. Damn, he looked good in his white jeans. Keith gave the valet his ticket to pick up his car. I assumed that he must've gotten a rental earlier. We rode off in a convertible Ford Mustang. The day was spent sightseeing while talking and laughing about everything from reality television to silly politics. It was so easy to talk to him. I learned more about him but not enough to read him. Most men were predictable, which gave me the upper hand, but not Keith. He was unlike any man I'd ever met. He is mysterious and I liked the challenge.

We pulled into a local park and sat on a bench, secluded from the rest of the park's occupants. Oddly, there were no kids or families there, just a few people sparingly walking by. He rolled up a blunt of Loud. We took hit after hit as we watched the birds fly by in search of food. I listened intently while Keith told me about his artist, businesses, and trifles of women. He was cracking up at some of the stories I told him of some of the lames in my past. Our talk about the past and future dreams revealed that we are just two people drifting through life waiting on the right person to come along and nurture our potential. The games we run on other people are not needed on each other. We could just be ourselves. High as fuck, we drove back to the hotel in slow motion, or so it seemed to me. Keith decided to order room service and a bottle of wine.

While we waited, I took a shower. When I came out of the bathroom, Keith was setting up the food. He played an R&B playlist via Spotify through his phone's speaker. When he turned around, we made eye contact. It was something about the look he gave me. Or maybe it was the way he licked his lips when he saw me in my sheer romper. Keith drew closer to my face, closed in toward my lips, and kissed me. His lips were so soft, and his hands touched me in all the right places. He kissed my neck and slowly pulled the romper down past my breast.

As he took my left breast in his hand, he whispered in my ear, "Are you sure, Kim?"

I began to moan. "Yes, I'm positive."

We made it to the bed. He pulled the romper down to the floor, and I laid back on the bed, watching him undress. His milk chocolate skin looked edible. He leaned down and kissed my stomach, spreading my legs. He took his tongue and slid it from my belly button to my clitoris. He licked and swirled his tongue around my private areas until I came multiple times.

"Mmmm. Ooooh! YES," I screamed and moaned in octaves.

Each time, I thought it was the last time, but he would do this little thing with his tongue that would make me cum again. I arched my back, grabbed his head, and rolled my pussy slowly in his mouth. When he thought I'd had enough, he rose to his feet. I felt his hard dick touch my thigh as he climbed on top of me. We kissed as I tasted my body's sweet nectar. I motioned him to turn over, so I could get on top. I had to return the favor. I straddled him, kissing his chest simultaneously.

Once he groaned a few times, I made my way down his torso until my lips met the tip of his penis. I felt his body exhale. I teased him, licking the shaft of his dick up and down. Then I opened my mouth and let his dick slide to the back of my throat. Making sure it was wet and sloppy, I guided him in and out slowly. While caressing his balls, I started to go faster with my mouth until he couldn't take it any longer.

"FUCK!" he cried out in a husky whisper.

I climbed back on top of him, took his dick in my hand, and guided him into what we both wanted. He grabbed both sides of my hips and thrust upward. At that moment, it felt like his dick was touching my soul. I had been pretending with men for so long that I'd almost forgotten what a real orgasm felt like. I wanted to make this one count. Our rhythms matched in every position we chose. The only one he couldn't defeat me in was doggy style. I rolled back on his dick that last time, and he pulled me from behind up to his chest and whispered.

"I'm about to cum, Kim."

I leaned back down with my ass in the air. He put his left hand under my stomach and pulled my ass closer. He grabbed my hair with his right and began to pump harder and deeper.

"Oh, shit!" Keith hollered, louder this time. I felt his cum explode inside of me, and I came with him. We both lay in a spooning position until our stomachs growled in unison.

We got up and showered together. After we got to enjoy each other's bodies again in the shower, we pigged out on room service food, listening to old school R&B, killing yet another bottle of wine. Feeling tranquil, I laid in his arms all night. *Damn, how the fuck did one breakfast date end up here? And why the hell did I let this man's sex get me out of my comfort zone?*

Chapter Six: The Get Back

I regretted sending Kim back home, but I couldn't afford to let our time together deter me from what I came to Texas to do. If I'd let her stay longer, she would've definitely knocked me off my game. I hoped that I held her attention enough that we could hook up when I got back to Atlanta. She seemed to be a cool girl. I liked the fact that she held her own while she was here and didn't ask me for anything. Most chicks see that a nigga has money, and they be pocket watching, trying to see what they can get out of him. In my opinion, a woman that doesn't ask for anything deserves it all.

I tried to call Kim at least once a day because our conversations were long and fulfilling. I was revealing things to her that I had never thought I would tell any woman. She was so easy to talk to. She turned me on intellectually and I had to admit, my dick got hard just thinking about her and the night we had sex. She had all the right moves. No woman had ever made me want to cum with a slow head game. I've had some good sex in my life, but Kim got that love making sex. That bid in Coffee County State prison provided me with a lot of time to reflect on my life and women. I had learned that sex was not the determining factor of love. In my book, loyalty was more important than anything. You could get sex anywhere, anytime. I hoped that Kim was the exception to the rule because I'm fucking with her the long way.

I was lying low in Houston with Candi. It had been complicated, to say the least. Candi was the simplest broad I had ever met. She was a daddy's girl, and her family ran her life. She kicked it to me like she had her shit together but in reality, all she was good for was keeping a nigga books fat and doing errands for me while I was locked down. After being out here for three weeks, I found out this bitch didn't know anything except what someone else told her. It worked out in my favor since she thought I was broke, and wanted me to get on my feet. Her simple ass just didn't know that once I left Texas, I was never coming back her way. I just told her what she wanted to hear to keep the shit drama free. She convinced her father to give her money for some hair business she was trying to start. I talked her into letting me flip it. However, she did get a few bundles of hair to test out. I truly hoped she got something going with the business because she wasn't getting shit from me.

However, twenty-five bands from a bitch I wasn't attracted to was priceless. She didn't turn me on in any way.

I'd seen her come home from work too many times and go to bed without taking a bath. My biggest pet peeve was a nasty bitch. A woman should stay fresh at all times. If I had to tell one to take a bath, I was done. In three weeks, she had only got this dick one time, but I let her give me that sorry ass head damn near every day. I dipped out every day to hit the streets in search of what I had really come to Texas for. A plug.

***

Two months later

I came to Texas with a little over a hundred grand, which was my cut on the play we did on the South Carolina niggas. I had been going to a day labor warehouse that employed mostly Mexicans. Niggas who bought bricks knew that if they wanted a plug, they'd have to come to Texas. After working on this bullshit job for two months, I listened and took notes about this guy named Romero Santana, in El Paso. I didn't let on that I spoke fluent Spanish to my new friend Jose until he set up the buy from Romero. I impressed him during our meeting. Most people were surprised when a nigga spoke another language, so I knew that would help wow Romero and gain a little of his trust.

I spent the last few days waiting on JRock and Trey to come up with their portion of the money we needed to make this deal go through. Today was the day. I had turned my hundred grand into one hundred and seventy-five grand by selling small weight. That amount included the money from Candi. But them two-trick ass niggas fucked up a good share of their money, trying to take care of those money hungry ass hoes in Atlanta's strip clubs. Regardless, they had met the amount needed for the deal. Those niggas probably terrorized Atlanta with home invasions and shit, but that wasn't my business. I stopped doing that shit a long time ago. I made a promise to God when I was in prison that I wouldn't do another home invasion. It always involved innocent people that didn't have anything to do with a nigga or his money, and there was always a chance that things could quickly go left. I didn't want to be on the 11 o'clock news again for killing an innocent mother or child just for some nigga's cash. The system hides your ass for being young dumb and stupid, but I'd grown from that stupid shit.

What really retired me from the robbery game was the last mission Trey, JRock, and I pulled. I remembered it like it was yesterday. Trey got shot in his leg, chest, and arm. Fortunately, the bullets missed his major organs, and he successfully pulled through, but I couldn't shake the scene out of my mind. It could have been avoided if JRock had done more homework on the nigga we were jacking. JRock always geeked up on all types of pills and his mind be on go at all times but shit be causing him to spaz out sometimes. That type of shit can cause all kinds of fuck ups in the streets. Trey and I tried to keep his head on straight as much as we could because he is our boy. Therefore, when he did get into some shit, we were down to help him out of it by any means necessary. It was our Bro code.

On this particular fuck up, some young cats robbed him in the Blue Flame parking lot for a kilo and jewelry, and he wanted revenge. He told us the guy was just a random dude shacking up with one of his baby mamas, but he could stand to be robbed. He thought it would be a simple in and out job, but he didn't know the guy had shooters in the house.

All JRock knew was Trey, and I would be down for getting some money, and we had his back on a sweet lick. He also knew I got up at the crack of dawn and that Trey didn't mind walking a nigga's kids back in the house to encourage him to give up the loot. Seeing Trey's big ass hovering over your daughter would make any nigga shit bricks if they thought they'd see her get raped in front of them over some street shit. So, most niggas would comply and give up the stash. JRock assured us the shit was sweet, and we wouldn't have any issues. I was a little hesitant because JRock stayed on some wild shit, but Trey had his eyes on some new rims for his whip, and he was committed before I could object. I was out voted, and back then, we never did a job without all three of us.

We got up at 4:30 am and dressed in all-black jump out gear. We drove the utility van we purchased for missions such as this. It was an old white van that didn't stick out to any neighborhood-watch hero. We watched the house and the surrounding houses until the lights inside started to pop on. That meant that people were up getting ready for work and school. Doing a home invasion in a black neighborhood early in the morning had its perks since nobody was looking out the windows. Plus, it was still dark outside, which limited eyewitnesses. Trey and JRock snuck up to the side of the front door and hid behind bushes. I went to the back door and posted up near the trash cans but sat close enough to hear the commotion inside. We maintained our positions and waited.

The dude walked his two daughters out the door and stood on the front porch, watching them walk down the steps. As the two girls' feet hit the bottom steps, Trey and JRock grab them by the neck, pointing guns to their heads. The dad's first instinct was to reach for his gun, but he remembered that he was wearing a fucking robe and didn't have his piece on him. He knew what time it was, so in a defeated stance, he waited for JRock's instructions.

"Walk slowly back into the house," JRock demanded.

As he and Trey walked up the steps, he handed Trey the other girl while he grabbed the dude's arms and walked him inside, gun pointing to the back of his head. Once everyone made it inside the living room, JRock proceeded to tie them up. I could hear the racket from outside. I wondered if everything was okay, but Trey came to the back door to give me the signal to come in. JRock told us the money and dope were hidden in the hallway's bathroom floor. As Trey and I passed the trio lying face down on the floor, I saw JRock lifting one of the girls' skirts. The father threatened to kill him if he touched either of his daughters. Tears flooded the man's eyes. I didn't know if it was out of fear that he would have witnessed JRock raping his daughter, or the thought that he had slipped up in the streets and karma was on his ass. Either way, he couldn't do a damn thing about it now because reality was happening right in front of him.

Trey entered the bathroom first. As soon as he stepped in the door, a bitch fired on him from the shower. I heard the shots and immediately pointed my gun in that direction, firing my 9mm. I never saw the person's face, but I remembered seeing bright red nail polish and a Daisy Duck tattoo on the wrist before they fell limp from behind the shower curtain, after the release of the gun. I yelled to JRock to help me to get Trey out of there. Trey gagged for air but was able to stagger as we carried him out. Luckily, we managed to get him to the van without anyone noticing. In the hood, when people heard gunshots, they weren't getting themselves involved if they didn't need to. We laid Trey in the back and pulled off.

JRock asked, "Did you get the money?"

I replied, "Hell no, do you see our boy back there, shot da fuck up? We goin' to Grady, fuck that money."

He replied, "Let me out. I'm goin' back. We need that cash homie".

I pulled over, and he jumped out and ran back down the street. I didn't think twice about it because, in my mind, I knew there was no sense in leaving the cash and dope. I kept Trey occupied, talking to him as we hit 85-N to Grady Hospital.

I pulled into the emergency parking deck and yelled for help. The Emergency Trauma team put Trey on a gurney and whisked him away. I told the nurse that he was shot, and in the commotion of them shouting at each other, I eased my way back out of the entrance door. I heard someone in the distance say, "Hey sir, we need to talk to you." but I jumped in the van and left.

Trey knew I had to leave him before the cops showed up, and we both knew not to say anything to the police. I knew that the guy and his daughters wouldn't be saying anything either because JRock wasn't going to let them live to do so.

Later that day, I found out my assumptions were right. After loading up the money and dope in the guy's car, JRock ushered the two girls and their dad into the trunk before he dropped the cash and dope off. Then he drove to a lake down in Lagrange, Georgia, opened up the trunk, and shot three bullets in each of their heads. He made sure they were dead, then closed the trunk, wiped the car down, put it in neutral, and let it roll into the lake. I picked him up at a truck stop twelve hours later and we went to divide the take. Then went to Trey's mom's house to wait on updates concerning his recovery. I knew that would be the last robbery that I'd do. I'd helped JRock revenge for too many people over things that could have been avoided. It always left a bad taste in my mouth to see innocent people get killed over something they didn't know anything about. I still have nightmares about one particular hit, resulting in killing two females. Some nigga had stolen Jay's car, and me and Trey were down for the get back.

We followed the dude's sister, for about a week, hoping to catch the nigga slipping. We were about to give up when we saw a nigga pulling up to the house in JRock's stolen ride with a different paint job. We waited for the dude to get out, but he didn't. Two women walked out of the house, and JRock jumped out of the car and started fucking firing on them. Trey and I were shocked. That wasn't the plan, but we couldn't leave our boy out there by himself after it started. I saw the dude hopping out of the car, attempting to fire back at us, but it was too much firepower, and he was outnumbered. He ran for his life through a path on the side of the house. I remembered seeing the back of his head disappearing through bushes as he limped. I think he was hit in the leg or ankle.

The cops had no leads and didn't bother searching for any. I guess the dude was a known drug dealer in the area, so those country cops ruled all black murders as drug related cases. They didn't spend any time investigating. At the time, I was eighteen-years-old. I didn't think anything of it. It was just a day in the life of the streets. I often wonder, why JRock fired on the chick and why he was so pressed about that damn car, but we never discussed it. The shit was fucked up though.

I'm glad JRock isn't with Trey right now, because Trey was on his way to Texas with the funds to pay the new plug and we don't need any problems. I had just gotten off the phone with JRock, and he told me that Trey rented a car with a fake ID and had left days before heading to Texas with the money we needed to seal the deal. I told Romero that I could buy twenty bricks at the price he gave me, which was twenty-five grand per unit if he agreed to front me twenty. He agreed. With these new prices, the crew and I were about to flood Atlanta. Niggas in Georgia are paying thirty to thirty-two grand per unit. Tomorrow I was going back to Atlanta, and we were about to run our checks up.

If I could do this three times per month, I would clear over two hundred and sixty thousand a month. This was my type of shit. I eat, my niggas eat, and the plug stays happy. It's a done dollar. All I had to do was convince Candi to rent another car and drive us to Atlanta. Then send her ass back with absolute quickness.

Chapter Seven: New Friends

Daisy and I were headed to the hair salon when she got a call from her cousin from Texas. She was headed to the ATL, and she wanted to hang out with us this weekend. The Drake concert was where every female in Atlanta was going to be. We had three front row tickets, compliments of Daisy's husband, Greg. He hosted his own segment at V103, and his connections kept us in the hottest spots in Atlanta. So, it was only fitting that when family came to visit, we showed them the time of their lives. Everybody loved the Atlanta nightlife, and Daisy and I knew our way around the scene. We didn't go out often, but when we did, it was a 5-star event. This weekend was no different. We were sparing no expense. Limo, *Westin Suites*, and of course I went to Phipps Plaza and copped us the hottest Saint Laurent and Tom Ford outfits.

After our hair, nails, and eyebrows were done, we headed to Daisy's to plan out the last few details of the night. We meet Greg in the driveway as we pull in. After he instructed us to be on our best behavior, he headed out. Greg would be busy promoting V103 all night, so he encouraged Daisy to have a girl's night out. As long as he thought that Daisy was with a friend, she wouldn't be lonely without him around. If only Greg knew that Daisy was *far* from lonely. She asked me to book a separate room so that she and her lil' boo thang could have a rendezvous after the concert and after-party. I was happy to do it because Daisy had gotten me out of many jams in the past. If it wasn't for her, I'd probably be dead by now. One of these niggas would have killed me for sure.

I never asked her anything about her marriage, but I did know that she wasn't happy with Greg. The only reason she hadn't divorced him yet was that they had a child. So, if having a lil' boo thang kept her smiling, I was okay with it. Besides, I'm sure Greg had pussy in his face on the regular. All the radio personalities did. They lived in the strip club and swore that they were in there having business luncheons, but talking business with ass shaking in your face was nearly impossible, especially for a thirsty lame like Greg.

"Daisy, I hope this cousin of yours is on our level. We don't need anybody crampin' our style or being a tattle-tell afterward." I didn't fuck with too many females, so I wasn't crazy about creating fake friendships. The less a bitch knew about you, the better. So, I didn't need any more new friends. One thing I knew, a bitch is okay with you as long as she thought she was better than you or had more, but as soon as a hatin' female got a sense that you were doing or had a little more than her, she'll surely start that jealous shit. Either she disrespects you by pushing up on your man or start spreading rumors. As the saying goes, *when the hate doesn't work, they start telling lies.*

"Oh girl, she's cool. She's just one of them daddy's girls gone wild after they get to college. Now, she's all turnt out by these simple niggas. She's the type to do anything for a man. Always taking care of one by giving up her checks and shit. The last time I checked, she was shacked up with a nigga who just got out of jail. She met him on his work detail in prison, and she swears he is the love of her life." Daisy laughed at that. "I think that's who she's traveling here with. He has family here or something. Gurl, who knows. I'm not trying to think about her. Let me see this dress you got me, bitch," Daisy said as she started tearing into my bags in search of her outfit.

"Owwee, Kimmie, this dress is the bomb. You know my taste so well. My body ain't made for that ratchet shit. I like classy stuff. You should definitely be a stylist," she said.

"You welcome, girl. You know I got you. I can't have my best friend looking like a groupie out here in these streets. You will be turning heads in that dress honey! But do your folks at least know how to party?" I pressed. "Lord, please say she knows how to dress," I said under my breath while Daisy went to try on her dress. We surely didn't need a busted thirsty chick running with us tonight.

"If she acts up, we are throwing her ass to the curb," I shouted. We both burst out laughing.

"I know that's right, gurl, but we may have to do a makeover because that girl has never been into fashion. Her mom could never get her to wear dresses when we were little," Daisy shouted from the bathroom.

"Well, I brought my makeup case and some extra outfits if we need to make a miracle happen," I reminded.

"As a matter of fact, let me see where this trick is at. She said she made it to Georgia a few hours ago, so she should be here soon," Daisy announced.

Daisy got her phone and started typing with her extralong red nails. I looked toward the bathroom, and I got a glimpse of her naked reflection in the mirror. I now understood why Daisy was so self-conscious of her body. She had terrible scars on her abdomen. I wouldn't dare ask her about them. I turned away so she wouldn't notice me staring.

I heard her talking on the phone with someone then tapping the screen to hang up.

"Okay. She said she is dropping her man off now and she's on the way. So, we good," Daisy said while heading to get dressed.

I'm glad she is not bringing her man. We really don't need any new friends or scrubs tagging along killing our vibe. My only concern was about these Atlanta streets that we were about to tear up tonight. I couldn't wait to see Drake's fine ass sing to me. Tonight, would surely be one for the books.

Chapter Eight: The Life

When Candi got out of the car to pay for the gas, Trey barked, "Man, where you find this crazy girl at? Bruh, she almost got us caught with all this shit. Her ass was speeding for no damn reason and doing all that talking about nothing. I've been cracking up back here listening to y'all. Shit, she almost made us catch a case. I was low key scared as fuck, bruh. But that was G shit she did though. Aye yo, why does she keep callin' you, Kendrick?"

"Bruh, this chick crazy as fuck. She doesn't know my real name. I just used her to come up in Texas, but you right. I'm glad her dad's got connections because our ass would've been dead in the water when the police pulled us over. This is the last time she'll ever see my ass. Her ass done, bruh. Once I get my shit out of this car, I'm changin' my number, so she won't be able to contact me again. Why you think I told her to drop us off at College Park train station to pick up my car? I don't need her to GPS my whereabouts or doubling back. This bitch is a done dollar, my nigga," I confirmed as we laughed and dapped it up.

"Man, you be finding some weird ass chicks. I told you about messin' with them dense, high-class ass bitches. They can't be trusted when shit really matters," Trey said.

Trey never liked girls outside of Carver Homes. He was always preaching about how chicks outside the hood couldn't be trusted and how they would snitch on you if the cops put their asses in an interrogation room. I wasn't worried about any of that, least of all from Candi's ass. She was crazy, but she wasn't stupid. She gets some brownie points for keeping a level head. When the cops pulled us over, she asked Siri to start recording and Facetime her dad. As soon as the cop acknowledged her father, we were free to go without incident.

***

The concert was lit as fuck. Bitches were on point in every direction, and niggas were not half-stepping. Atlanta's elites were out, and the thirst was real. I saw a couple of outfits and purses I had sold to people, but I didn't front on my customers when I saw them out because my clientele were business owners or corporate types. How they bought their clothes is nobody's business anyway. I just gave a smile and nod as I passed them. We had mutual respect.

Drake did his thing on stage, and I never solo danced so much in my life. Once we finished killing the afterparties, we headed back to the hotel. We told Candi that she would be bunking with me because Daisy was expecting Greg later. There was no reason to tell her the truth because the less she knew, the better. I really wasn't feeling her that much, but since I didn't have company coming, it was cool for us to be roomies for the night, and I could use this time to pick her brain and see if I could pull her in on some business in Texas. My credit card crew traveled to major cities to shop, so knowing someone in each town was a plus. Who knew, her simple ass could have connections in Texas.

I booked Daisy's room on a different floor so no one would catch her boo going into the room. I'd never met him, nor did I want to. Even if Greg came looking for her, he wouldn't know which room she was in because I booked the room with one of the fake IDs, but Daisy and I had an alibi in case Greg did stop by to check on us. I'd text or call her to signal that Greg was in the room, and I'd say that she went to the car to get her purse. So, when she staggered to the room, she would have her purse and keys in hand. Luckily, we never had to use the plan because Greg never checked on us when we went out. He probably had his own side piece ducked off somewhere in Atlanta. I often wondered why Daisy had a side piece because Greg seemed to be a good guy, but who knew. All niggas had a level of craziness hidden from the world. Wives had to put up with it or maneuver around it; girlfriends and side pieces didn't. I guess Daisy was maneuvering right now, because she is probably getting her back blown out, but I'll never know because we have a "Don't Ask, Don't Tell" policy. I stayed out of her business, and she stayed out of mine. We had each other's back, and that's all that mattered.

When Candi and I entered the suite, she jumped her ass straight in the bed. I headed to the bathroom and filled the tub with warm water and lavender bath beads. I don't care how turnt up I was, I had to wash the night off me. While the water was running, I poured three glasses of champagne and turned on Pandora. I drank out of each glass and left lipstick smudge on them just in case Greg did stop by, so it looked like all three of us were in the room at one time or another.

Candi was lying down watching reruns of *Love and Hip Hop Atlanta*. I don't know why people believed that these reality shows depicted what really happens in Atlanta. The only storyline that was remotely true was Mama Dee being a pimp back in the day. The rest of that bullshit is for ratings.

"So, how do you like the ATL so far?" I asked Candi as I walked in front of the TV to get her attention.

"Gurl, I love it! If I can land a job, I want to move out here," she shrieked.

She told me that her dad was a well-known politician in Texas and how she wanted to get out from under his shadow, so she wanted a fresh start in a new city. I asked her what she did for a living. She told me that she just started a hair extension company and worked for her dad as a property manager.

"I have a client who manages apartments. I can ask her if she has anything open if you're interested." I hadn't figured out if I liked Candi or not, but I offered just to be polite.

"Girl, that would be great! I need a job asap because I plan on getting an apartment for me and my boyfriend, Kendrick. I won't be staying with Daisy and Greg long, "she blurted out.

I didn't know why she felt the need to tell me all that, but I just nodded my head and smiled. I continued the conversation, "Oh yeah, Daisy mentioned your man was here. What does he do?" I asked nonchalantly as I ran into the bathroom to turn the water off.

"He just got an interview with the City of Atlanta Watershed Department," she said proudly.

She met him a year ago when she came to Georgia to intern at one of her father's friend's companies. But three months ago, he came out to stay with her in Texas, hoping to find steady work, but it didn't work out. He got a temp job at a manufacturing plant to generate some income, but it wasn't much. Translation: she took care of him until he got homesick and wanted to come back to Atlanta. She came back to Atlanta with him in hopes of him asking her to stay. This girl was *so* delusional. As much as I tried showing interest, I grew tired of hearing her talk about this dude. It's beginning to sound like the typical Atlanta fuck nigga shit. He is trying to live off her simple-minded ass.

"I fell in love with him, and I think he's the one," she bragged.

Bitch, I didn't ask you all that but, okay, I thought, rolling my eyes. Daisy already told me she met the nigga on his prison detail when she was here in Georgia last summer.

I just say, "That's cool. He sounds nice. I wish you two much happiness."

But I was really thinking, *gurl, that nigga used you up, and you better watch out if he gets that city job because those city workers are known in the ATL for running game.* They flashed their big overtime paychecks and are always bragging about their good benefits. Simple chicks fell for it hook, line, and sinker but ended up being ran through and looking crazy. Those type of niggas were either married or living paycheck to paycheck. Meaning they work to pay car notes on cars they used to flex with. Candi started staring at her phone with that same confused look she had earlier. Although I wanted to know what was up with her demeanor, the bubbles were calling my name. I walked away from our conversation and into the bathroom.

I slipped in the tub, sunk my body underneath the bubbles, and let Anthony Hamilton relax me, with his smooth soulful voice. As I hummed along to *Point of it All*, a text message interrupted my relaxation. I reached up and grabbed my phone. It was Keith.

Keith: GN/ GM Beautiful. I can't wait to see you. Lunch Tomorrow? - Keith

Me: I'm looking forward to seeing you too, Mr. Thomas. By the way, did you get everything squared away in Texas? What time do you land tomorrow?

Keith: Yeah, it's all good. I thought about you a lot. I got something for you. I took a redeye. I just touched down tonight.

Me: Oh yeah. Cool. What do you have for me?

Keith: It's a surprise. See you tomorrow. GN. This my new number so lock it in! Meet you at Buckhead Diner at 12.

Keith: OK, can't wait. GN.

I put the phone back on the nightstand and got back into Anthony, only to be interrupted by another text. It was Jaylen.

Jaylen: WYD?

I didn't respond. I knew Greg probably told him I was out with Daisy. It might've been a trap, so I didn't want to get into that. Besides that, I didn't like being summoned by him. That was my job, and right now, my pockets were straight, so I didn't have time to fool with Jaylen. I needed to relax and get my head together. Before I saw Keith tomorrow, I wanted to hit Lenox to get some orders. That was one of the reasons I chose to meet him in Buckhead.

I hopped out of the tub and stepped in the shower to rinse the soap off. After the warm water cleansed me from head to toe, I oiled my body down and put on a bathrobe. Candi was sound asleep with that phone glued to her hand when I walked into the room. I covered her up and placed the phone on the nightstand. Glancing at her phone, I noticed the *message not sent* icon. I didn't bother to read the text.

***

When we pulled into Daisy's driveway, I saw Jaylen's truck parked next to mine. He and Greg were lounging by the pool.

Greg spoke first, "Oh, look what the cat drug in. Good morning, ladies."

We laughed as we girls took a seat around the glass table. Greg looked surprised to see Candi with us. He walked up to her and stood squarely in front of her.

"Hey, Candi. I didn't know you were in town," Greg said. I noticed his sexual undertone but brushed it off as Greg being Greg.

Daisy interrupted before Candi could speak, "Babe, I told you she was coming yesterday morning on your way to work. That's why we needed a third ticket. Remember you were on the phone with the station?"

Greg never knew whether he was going or coming. Without Daisy, he would've been lost in the world. Greg was nerdier than Steve Urkel. I didn't understand why he was friends with Jaylen. I guess opposites attract, but Jaylen wasn't a good friend to Greg or anyone else. All he did was talk about how he helped this person or that person. Jaylen was the most arrogant nigga I had ever met. He was also ill tempered. He just snapped sometimes. I'm glad I was never around him long enough for it to bother me. The only thing I admired about him was his hustle and independence. I was impressed that he had his own place. As a matter of fact, he had a couple of places to lay his head at night. He'd never asked me for shit --not even when he went to jail for three months on a probation violation. He called me a few times from jail, but he put his own money on his books and Securus phone account. He allowed one of his homeboys to hold his cell phone while he made things happen on the street. I got paid just for conversation. Every time I got off the phone with him, I got a Cash App for a hundred dollars. Most small-time niggas got behind bars and couldn't afford noodles. I despised that shit. If you knew you were in the game and understood the consequences, you needed to prepare for them. When you're in the game, having bond money and a lawyer on standby is a must. Period.

I happened to have met my attorney in the courtroom when I was at Calvin's hearing. He was a sexy chocolate 5'7 specimen dressed for the Gods. I caught him in the cafeteria when we were on lunch break. I bumped into him on purpose.

"That is a nice Brooks Brothers suit. And you are walking the walk in them Gucci loafers," I politely said.

He smiled and used his best man voice, "Why, thank you."

I knew he was gay from the start because he did a little curtsy and twirl after I gave him the compliment. Only a confident gay man would sway like that in Gucci loafers.

I extended my hand to shake his, "Hello, my name is Kimberly Davison."

"Hello, Miss Davison. I'm Timothy Evans, Attorney at Law, and yassss aren't I fly today?" We laughed.

Since that day, Tim and I had become the best of friends. I had become his personal stylist, so to speak. I shopped for him with the faux credit cards, and he compensated me well. He was knowledgeable about everything, and he knew to answer my call no matter what.

I never know when this little credit card shit will go left. If I end up behind bars, Tim will inherit two teenagers until I or Calvin get out. That's how close we had become. After meeting him, Tim agreed to work on Calvin's appeal pro bono as a favor to me. Tim was gay, but he didn't push his lifestyle off on anybody, not that I care one way or the other. I've never seen him with his partner though. He is secretive as hell about that part of his life, and he lets people know all the time ain't shit sweet about him. He had a lot of hood in him too. He has a little saying he loves to blurt out when somebody tests his gangsta: "The hood is in me, not on me." I guess that's why we click. He is just a cool dude. Tim was the one who put me on to Peter. They were rivals in his office, and he needed Peter to be distracted for a while, so he could one-up him in some case they were fighting for. Let's just say Tim won the case.

Jaylen walked towards me and asked if I wanted to get something to eat. I declined and told him that I had to get home to my kids. I couldn't let him mess up my day because I had plans with Keith.

"Call JRock, later, Aight," he told me before leaving for his car.

I didn't know what had gotten into Jaylen, but he had a different look in his eyes. It looked as if he were starting to catch feelings for me, but I could never be with Jaylen. Hell, he didn't even know me. He thought I was a sweet innocent country girl who didn't know anything about his hustle. I waited until he pulled off, then said my goodbyes to Daisy, Greg, and Candi. Then hopped in my car and headed straight to Buckhead.

***

On route, Keith texted and said he was running late and asked if we could meet at one instead of twelve. That was cool with me. I could kill time and make a pit stop at Lenox and purchase the new CELINE bag for my customer.

I walked into Saks Fifth Avenue wearing a Chanel dress with matching pumps. The clerk asked if she could help me. I asked to see the new Nano Luggage CELINE bag.

"Oh yes! We just got them last week. Come, let me show you," she said with a big smile.

I learned that you could take the salesclerk's mind away from any red flags if you knew what you were talking about. I made it a ritual to look nice while I'm shopping. I never understood why boosters went to the mall looking any kind of way. Whenever you went into a designer store, you had to dress the part. No salesclerk would believe that a person was about to purchase a three thousand dollar bag wearing outdated Baby Phat or those God-awful PINK tights and slides. I admired the bag and told her to ring it up. I placed the Saks card on the counter along with the ID that read *Melissa Stephens*.

The clerk bagged it up and said, "Have a nice day, Mrs. Stephens."

I strutted out of the store with a smirk on my face. I had just earned a thousand bucks in fifteen minutes. I sold my items for half price, but I had to give Kawame a third of it. I had to stay on the up and up with Kawame. First, he saw everything we purchased with the cards. Second, I knew there were plenty of bitches that he could be fucking with on this play, but he chose to fuck with me, and I was loyal to him for that. Last week, he'd given me a Hollister card. I texted him and asked him if it was a go. He replied with a simple *yes*. I kept store cards such as that for myself and the twins because nobody checked for items there but kids. The high-end stores brought cash, so Kawame said we could keep the low-end store cards. I went and purchased the twins a shit-load worth of clothes, then headed to meet Keith.

***

When I drove up to the Buckhead Diner, I saw Keith sitting in his car on the phone. He immediately ended his call when he saw me. I don't know who he was talking to, but he was letting them know, what's in front of him is much more important. He got out of his car and opened my car door. Once we were seated, he asked, "You miss me?"

I laughed and said, "Well, of course."

"Lies you tell," he said and laughed.

We sat for about two hours, talking and catching up. For the first time, I looked past his beautiful eyes and sparkling white teeth. I listened to his soul. I don't know if I was horny as hell, but I really wanted to jump on his ass, but I refrained from acting on my impulses. I wanted to wait until the perfect time. Against my protocol, I shared some personal details of my life with Keith. I told him about the twins and their father being in prison and about Tashia's demise. It was too complicated to explain how I'd become the twin's mother in the aftermath, so I gave him the condensed version of the story and omitted telling him they weren't my biological kids. It was easy to talk to Keith because no matter how much I told him, he never judged me. I told him about my current hustle, and he told me about his dealings. However, neither of us disclosed how much money we were making. I couldn't believe that this nigga was on my level. He didn't care about what I was doing. So, I had nothing to lose by letting him into my life. I might as well let the walls down. We'd known each other for a few months, the sex was good, yet he wasn't sex craved. I decided that I'd keep Keith around for a while. I invited him to my house for dinner, and he accepted. The twins were at a friend's house, and I hadn't seen or heard from Tanya in a couple of weeks. I was beginning to worry about her. Even when she was on a drug binge, she found time to call me. I made a mental note to make time to look for her so she could come home.

Keith walked me to my car and made sure that I was securely inside. Before I left, he said, "Wait right here. I almost forgot to give you your gift." He ran to his car and jetted back with a gift bag in hand. I opened it and pulled out a receipt from my school. My tuition and books had been paid in full for the semester.

"Oh, my God! How did you? When did you? I can't believe this. Thank you so much!" I got out and hugged Keith. *It's the take charge game for me. His finesse game is almost better than mine. He is really making it hard for an ex and the next nigga. The life of a real hustler can't be out done.*

"Just make sure to send me an invitation to your graduation. Whether we're together or not." He planted a huge kiss on my lips. "I'll see you tonight, Miss Davison."

As I drove away, pondering what had just happened. Did that mean we were together? If so, I needed to change my lifestyle around to accommodate Keith's presence.

Chapter Nine: Seduced

After leaving Victoria Secrets, I stopped by Publix to grab the ingredients I needed for the romantic dinner I had planned for Keith and me. I hoped he was ready to be wined and dined because I planned to seduce him in every way tonight. When I got in the car, my phone buzzed. It was a text from Jaylen. *WYD?* I ignored it. He was really getting on my nerves. He seemed to want to talk or hook up every day. I didn't have time for his issues today. I didn't reply.

***

I washed the chicken and put it in the refrigerator to marinate while cleaning the house from top to bottom. I changed my bedsheets and made sure that every bathroom was fully stocked with toiletries. I would hate for someone to be in my bathroom taking a shit, and there's no toilet paper or hand soap in there.

After I made a bowl of Greek salad, I placed the baked potatoes and spinach-stuffed chicken breasts in the oven and took a shower. I moisturized my skin with cashmere lotions and sprayed on my Marc Jacobs perfume. I slipped on my new silk loungewear I bought earlier today. I was tempted to wear boy shorts and a tank top, but I opted for something classier. For some reason, men loved women wearing boy shorts around the house. I guess it was because their booty cheeks peeked out. Men and their silly fetishes. Oh, well. Keith wouldn't be getting boy shorts action tonight. This was grown woman business.

While I set the table with my Versace dinner plates and stemware, the doorbell rang. Keith arrived on time. I opened the door after he rang twice. I didn't want to seem desperate.

"Hello, Mr. Thomas. Come on in and make yourself comfortable. Dinner will be ready in a minute," I said, ushering him. I wanted the aroma of the kitchen to hit him in the face.

"Something smells good. Who do you have in here cookin?" he said with a slight chuckle.

"Oh, don't try me. I get down in the kitchen. Trust and believe you will want me to cook for you all the time, mister," I shot back.

"Yeah, right. All southern girls claim they can cook, but most of them can't boil water," he teased.

"Well, I'm not most girls, so you would definitely lose your money betting against me." We burst out laughing.

I gave him a quick tour of the house and escorted him to the living room while I checked on the food.

"Do you watch sports?" he yelled to the kitchen.

"Not really, but I cheer for Atlanta no matter what. It's the Falcons, Hawks, Braves, and United up in this camp. All day, every day," I boasted.

"That's what's up. I knew you were my kind of girl. Do you mind if I turn the game on," Keith asked?

"Of course, you can. The remote is on the coffee table."

I heard the TV come on as I walked off to the kitchen. It wasn't long before Keith made his disapproval for the game known.

"Look at this bullshit," Keith screamed.

I ran back into the living room and asked, "Is everything okay?"

"Oh, yeah. I'm sorry for shouting. These dirty ass Falcons just lost to the Saints," he said with disappointment.

"That's the Falcons for ya. Don't they play them again next month," I said and shook my head.

"Yeah, they do. And I hope they get it together by then too. For my pocket's sake," Keith confessed he gambled on the game.

"Yeah, I'm sure Author Blank hopes so too. Well, the food is ready whenever you want to eat," I replied to try and cheer him up. Food and sex seem to cheer any man up, after losing money, and Keith is about to get both.

"Okay, cool. I want to hit this blunt first. Your house is beautiful, and I know you don't smoke in here. I can step outside," he assumed.

"You assumed correctly. But you can smoke on the patio. It's screened in. Come on, I'll show you," I replied.

As we walked past my office, Keith noticed the chessboard I had set up.

"You play chess, Kim?" he asked.

"Yeah, I dabble in it a bit. Nawl, let me stop. I'm actually great at it. At least, I think so. As you can see, I'm in the middle of a game with myself right now. I'm stomped on a move that can save me a loss from myself," I replied. I giggled and continued walking towards the patio.

"I would love to beat you at a few games one day, " he said with confidence.

"Yeah, right. You definitely won't be winning, but you can try it," I boasted.

We sat out on the patio, drank a glass of wine, and smoked a blunt. After we finished, we went to the dining room table to eat. We talked and laughed about the Falcons losing, among other things. He enlightened me about his dreams of having his own record label. I told him of my dream of opening a chain of Tax offices. I elaborated on how I wanted to have training classes and bring young women in under the franchise umbrella and teach them the ropes. That way, they could venture out on their own. Ain't nothing like having your own cash flow. I see too many women out here depending on men to feed them. Hell, I know all too well how that shit can end in disaster. Keith and I agree to support each other on both dreams. Together we would be unstoppable partners.

Once I cleaned off the table, we went back on the patio. After another blunt, I was super buzzed. I laid back on the lounge chair and placed my feet on Keith's lap. He caressed my feet, moving his hand slowly up to my thighs. I closed my eyes and exhaled and moaned. He moved in closer and massaged my lower back. I opened my eyes and motioned him to come closer. We kissed until I felt his nature rise against my inner thigh. He stood up, and I unbuttoned his jeans, pulling them down to the floor. As he stepped out of them, I pulled the lounge dress over my head to expose my naked body.

In a sexy voice, he says, "Kim, you are so beautiful. I want you so bad right now."

While he stood in front of me, I took his penis in my hands and guided it to my mouth. He leaned his head back and moaned. He intertwined his fingers in my hair, looking down into my eyes as I looked up into his. We seduced each other for what felt like hours. Keith took my body to euphoric heights. Lord knows I needed this. He seemed to be equally pleased. After I came several times, I asked him to cum for me. Without hesitation, he came inside of my heavenly realm. We lay on the lounge sofa staring into space until we fell asleep.

I woke up around 2:00 am and found Keith still sleeping soundly beside me. I shook him and his eyes fluttered open. I let him know that I was taking a shower and asked if he wanted to get in the bed. He agreed and followed me upstairs to the master bathroom. I turned the shower on and hopped in. I told him where the towels and extra toothbrushes were, but before I could finish my sentence, Keith opened the shower door and eased behind my soapy body. We were intimate once again while the warm water cascaded over our bodies until we both reached ecstasy once again. My knees were shaking uncontrollably. Keith eased me down enough to catch my balance. We stood in each other's arms allowing the water to rinse the sex off. Keith finished the job by soaping the loofah and then bathing me. Then proceeded to bathe himself. After rinsing off, we stepped out of the shower, dried off, and brushed our teeth. I disliked the smell of weed on my breath, and I assumed Keith did too. We climbed into my king-sized bed and Keith pulled me close to his naked body and cuddled me. He was indeed tearing down the walls I'd fought so hard to keep in place. He felt good and I could get used to him being around.

The next morning, I woke up to breakfast aromas. I usually don't sleep as blissfully when I have company, but Keith got up and cooked breakfast before I cracked an eye. I walked downstairs and made my way to the kitchen. He had a whole spread laid out for me. He kissed me good morning and told me he had to be somewhere, and he would call me later. I was cool with that because I needed to hit the malls. I walked Keith to the door.

He kissed me again and whispered in my ear, "You boil water just fine, Miss Davison." With a smile, he gave me a wink and walked to his car. My cheeks were redder than a bouquet of roses as I grinned ear to ear. I don't know what the future holds, but right now, I'm feeling Keith.

I walked back into the house and went to my office to check my emails and make a few calls. While on my phone, I noticed the pieces on my chess board had been moved.

Keith made the move I needed to checkmate. I shook my head, chuckling. That man was something else. He's doing all the right things.

Chapter Ten: The Game

Our team was in place, and the dope had been distributed. So, all Trey, JRock, and I had to do was sit back and let the money roll in. We made the game look easy, but being a Boss takes hella talent. Those forty units sold out as soon as I got back to the ATL. Niggas were in love with the quality of the product. When the shit is this good, it practically sells itself. I already got Romero's money and time to put it in the air to hand it over to him.

I contacted this cool TSA chick, I know. Sherri from Carver Homes and she looks out for her people. For a fee of course. I needed to know when she was working to get the money through airport security and head to Texas. I don't want to keep Romero waiting any longer than I have to. A good turn around is considered good business, especially in this game. I wanted Kim to go with me, but I couldn't figure out how to make another play with her in the car driving back. So, I took my homegirl Tara. I didn't want Kim to get caught up in no shit with me. Plus, Kim was busy with school, and she would be tied up this week with her twins. I couldn't keep her off my mind. She was the answered prayer that I prayed for while I was in prison. I wanted and needed a woman who didn't judge or try to change me. I had many skeletons in my closet, and I was still putting some in, but nevertheless, I wanted true love. I needed my future wife to have some understanding of the game and be the peace I needed to build our empire.

It's fucked up that her kids' dad was in prison, but his loss is my gain. I'm not a hater, by any means, but a nigga had to understand that a chick could only wait for so long before moving on with her life. I knew she took the kids to see him every weekend, but she assured me nothing was going on with them. Plus, he was serving a life sentence, so she was fair game. I didn't like stepping on another man's toes, but it was life. Kim also shared that she missed her best friend, who was killed in a drive-by shooting fourteen years ago. Shit reminded me of all the friends and loved ones I'd lost over the years. This was a cruel world we lived in. Only the strong survive, and Kim and I were survivors, so we fit together. My goal was to keep a smile on her face forever.

Sherri gave me the specific day, instructions, and her price, five grand. Everything was a go. She would pull me out of the security line, pretending to do a random search. Then she'd take me into the searching room, wait until the plane was nearly loaded, and walk me out herself, then give the okay for me to board the plane. Shit, I wish she was in Texas so she could let the dope back in, but she was not with that. For some reason, she thought that she would get fired for missing a lump sum of money in a search and that dope was the only thing that would send her to jail. Hell, both would send her to jail. I just let her think what she wanted because I needed her on my team. The only thing I had to worry about was driving from Texas.

***

Romero was pleased with how quick the turn-around was. He put me on his FedEx delivery hustle. That way, I wouldn't have to drive back and forth to Texas. The dope would be delivered to an address in Atlanta. He also had a truck driver who had an Atlanta route so I would only have to fly out to give him his money. I would just have to supply addresses and names for the delivery. That wouldn't be a problem because I knew plenty of silly broads that would let me send the shit to their address.

As Tara and I drove through Texas, I thought about Candi. She probably had been blowing my phone up. I wondered how she reacted once she realized that she couldn't contact me anymore. Nevertheless, I hoped she was okay and made it back home safely. She was a nice girl; she just wasn't my type. She had no sense of who I was at the core. I ran so much game on her in prison, and she fell for any and everything. I could never love a woman who didn't have her own mind. Her parents had such a hold on her life that she had no say. A nigga like me needs a woman who can handle my business and hers if needed. Hell, I couldn't even bring myself to sleep with Candi on a regular basis. She turned me off, but she couldn't see it. No matter how much I avoided her, she would still try to have sex. I forced myself to cum just to end it. I lied and told her that my sex drive had dropped since I left prison, and I cum quick, and her giving me head was better because I could last longer. She believed it, so that was our thing. I let Candi leave my mind and texted Kim.

Me: Hey Beautiful. How are you? Be back tomorrow morning.

Kim: Driving to the prison. Call me when you get in. I got something to tell you.

Me: OK.

I wondered what Kim had up her sleeve, but I hoped it had something to do with me kissing her beautiful body again. Hell, she might be pregnant because I had been busting nuts in her all during sex. I just couldn't seem to pull out. I damn near slept in it last time. I smiled as I replayed the memory in my mind and laid my head back on the headrest to catch some Zzz's. Tara drove the speed limit, so I knew I was straight.

With my eyes half-closed, I said, "Take us home, T."

"I got it, homie." Tara put the car on cruise control. It felt like we were floating in the wind.

***

The girls loved seeing their dad. But now that they were becoming teenagers, I could see their frustration of choosing between visiting him and hanging with their friends. Calvin loved them more than anything. I hoped that they would continue to want to come to see him even after they are grown.

While the twins bought snacks from the vending machine, Calvin asked me how I was doing. I gave a quick overview of my life. Calvin was like my brother. He knew everything about me. He watched me grow from a little girl to the woman raising his kids. Since we were teenagers, he has always given me advice and told me to be careful in the streets. The things he'd seen in prison weren't pretty. He'd witness too many niggas coming through these prison doors with no remorse for having done a female wrong. He always said, *don't let a nigga trick you out of your life. Trick him out of his first.* I told him about Keith and that he was recently within these same walls. He seemed confused or intrigued. His eyes widened, and his nostrils flared.

"What's that nigga full name? Let me do some research on him, "Calvin insisted.

I gave him Keith's government name, and he immediately started laughing uncontrollably.

"It's a small world, lil sis. That nigga was in the same dorm as me. We used to call him Keith Sweat because that nigga would beg a female out of her panties and money. He's a cool cat, and he's about his paper. We still do a little business together. When you talk to that nigga, tell him I want some of my money back from all the chess games he beat me in, " he requested.

"So, he's a playa?" I asked.

He said, "Nawl, sis. You know when a nigga in here, he gotta do what he gotta do to survive and get at some pussy and money on the outside. He's a solid nigga, no doubt. I would tell you if he wasn't. He ain't no down low nigga either. He 'bout his money by any means necessary. He good people. He was down here on some humbug dope charge. Matter of fact, one of the lil niggas from my click in here had snitched on him in court, so Keith came to me like a man to handle that shit. I can respect that. I moved aside and let him handle his business. We've been cool ever since. Shiid, it's hard to find a solid nigga in this place. You know these prison walls can turn a nigga mind sideways. Keith is one of the ones who made it out of here with a new outlook on life."

Calvin looked to the sky as if he was praying to God or searching for answers from the clouds.

"I've evolved too. I see it in the way I view things these days." He said pensively, "Just the other day I was playing chess, and I looked over and noticed some young cats playing dice. They were laughing one minute and about to fight the next. I saw their beef coming long before it happened because of how they were talkin' to each other. These young guys have no respect for anyone, and I guess I didn't either in my younger days. You know I was an arrogant smart ass back in those days," he admitted. We laughed in unison at the thought because we both knew he was exactly that. Calvin was known for being a badass back in the day. He was getting money at a young age, so everyone knew not to fuck with him on any level, or they would be dealt with accordingly. He was also the class clown back then too. When he started jivin' a person, he would take them all the way out. He should have been a comedian because he used to have us cracking up.

He continued, "Their interaction was so powerful, sis because it symbolized the growth we go through down this road. Boys become men in here. Those guys are in the beginning stages of this journey, and their paths can go a million ways. They can only pray and hope that it goes in their favor. I'm glad to be alive to realize and see my weakness and my growth. Some guys are not as fortunate.

They die in here without ever living up to their true potential or even realizing it. The judicial system is designed to catch a young nigga in the early stages of his life, when he's not strong enough mentally to make the right decisions. Then they stick him in here, trying to institutionalize his mind, so he'll come back time and time again. Without a strong support system, very few men leave here better than they came. You and my girls have given me a reason to be better and I'm trying to recover my life, so I can come home with a sane mind.

"I forgive more easily now. Some shit is just not worth my time and energy and definitely not my freedom. My mentor taught me how to forgive in order to move forward. I have to forgive the nigga who killed the love of my life. You remember in court when they kept saying I plotted and killed the wrong man in revenge for my girlfriend's death? They said the dude wasn't even in town when Truffles was killed. So, he didn't kill her, and I supposedly murdered an innocent man. That shit is ironic, and it's been bothering me to this day because I didn't even kill the dude."

Calvin reminded me of how the judicial system fucked him over. *I remember how the cops claimed his fingerprints were all over the murder weapon, even though he testified and admitted he had bought the gun on the streets the day after the victim was shot. Some guy had approached him and offered to sell it to him because he knew he wanted revenge. Calvin thought he was buying a clean gun. Before he could even use it, he was arrested at the hospital while visiting the twins in ICU. The detective said they had gotten an anonymous tip, and they found the gun in his car. The system is so fucked up.*

"Lil sis, I was too young and dumb to even think that the gun had a body on it. I probably should be in here for a lot of shit I've done, but I shouldn't be in here for this shit. I had to forgive myself for letting Truffles and the twins down." Cal seemed to get misty-eyed, but I knew he would never shed a tear. I sucked back my tears as well and continued to listen to him continue to pour his heart out.

"But the muthafucka who killed her is still runnin' free. I haven't gotten a solid word about that nigga because I need to forgive him too. I've played that day in my head a million times, but I can't remember who I had done wrong. It all happened so fast; I didn't get a chance to see the nigga face. The only thing I did out of the ordinary that day was pick up that car at the paint shop. Truffle's brother won it in a crap game, and I bought it off him to give to Truffle, but I never got the chance. I haven't given up on findin' her killer, but these walls have a way of playing tricks on your mind. I've turned over a new leaf. If this appeal goes in my favor, I'll let God handle everything from now on. I never told you this, but Truffle cheated on me once, and it took everything in me to forgive her. So, if I was strong enough to do that for someone I loved, I'm strong enough to forgive a stranger," he admitted.

"Wait. Whaaat? Don't put that cheating shit on my best friend," I said, raising my right eyebrow.

He continued, "Yeah, she tried to have a lil side piece one time. I wasn't trippin' at first because I knew she had some growin' up to do, so I wanted her to explore her options. I was willin' to wait for her no matter how long it took." Calvin grinned as he talked and reminisced about the good old days. He was a few years older than Truffles and me, but something about her caught his eye. He fell madly in love with her at first sight. Everywhere we went, he showed up and made sure we were straight.

"But that day was different. I caught her sittin' outside her mama house in the car with some nigga from Atlanta, and I blacked out. I pulled that nigga out the car and beat the fuck out of him so quick. You know I was quick with it back then," he laughed. "I forgave her, though. And three months later, she told me she was pregnant. Matter of fact, she told me the night before she died. I was picking her and her mama up to go to the courthouse to marry her that morning," Tears fell from his eyes. All I'm saying is, if a man has been through these doors and comes out solid, he deserves a chance at happiness. This place has a way of teaching a man what he really needs and wants. Give Keith a chance. It's time for you to give love a try, sis. I hope I'm fortunate to find love again one day."

The guard motioned us to wrap up our visit. The twins made it back in time to talk to Calvin for a few more minutes. He spoke to them about school, boys and cautioned them to watch out for no good niggas that only wanted their bodies and not their minds. After ten more minutes, our time with Calvin was over.

I didn't know what to think about Calvin's news about Keith, but I erased it out of my mind for the moment and watched the twins end their visit with their dad. However, he had me thinking that Keith was trying to play me or had ulterior motives. Either way, I was not about to let it happen

Chapter Eleven: Candi

Damn, I hoped Kendrick didn't get locked up again because I hadn't heard from him since I dropped him off. Every time I tried calling him, his phone was not in service. I should've gotten his address, so I could check on him. I'm sure he missed me, because I sure as hell missed him. Daisy and Greg kept pressuring me to introduce him to them. I'd only been in Atlanta a few weeks, but I could tell they were wondering how long I was staying and if I even had a man.

I hated coming to my cousin's house because her husband was always looking at me funny. Last night, he peeked into the guest bedroom where I slept, stood there, and masturbated. I acted like I was asleep, but I saw him out of the corner of my eye, whacking away. I decided not to tell Daisy because she seemed so happy with him. I didn't want to be the cause of her broken home, so I just tried to stay distant.

I had to take my rental car to the airport, so I asked Daisy to take me, but she had an early salon appointment.

Kim was on her way to take me instead. Kim was cool, but she was one of them label hoes. I knew she thought I was a charity case because she tried to dress me up for the concert the other night. I never understood how and why chicks got dressed up every day. That shit looked uncomfortable. Shit, I wore flats as much as I could because me and heels didn't work well together. Kim and Daisy looked silly walking around the Mercedes Benz Stadium all night in six-inch heels.

I washed up in the sink and threw on jeans, a t-shirt, and Jordans. Kendrick hated when I wore sneakers, but hell, I liked them because they were comfortable, and I could walk faster in them. Since I wouldn't be seeing him today, I decided to rock them. I went downstairs to wait for Kim. I saw Daisy pulling out the driveway, but Greg's car was still parked. Damn, I thought he was gone already. I opened the refrigerator to grab some juice. As soon as I shut the door, Greg was standing in my face.

"Good morning," Greg said in a seductive voice.

"Go- Goo-Good morning," I replied in a frightened tone. "Kim is on the way to get me to take the car back. She should be pulling up now," I said, desperately looking out the doorway and praying to God that Kim was out there, but I knew she wasn't.

"Yeah, Daisy told me you may need a ride to the airport. I wish I could take you, but I have a promo for the station." Moving in closer, his penis brushed against my butt as he passed by. My phone vibrated on the counter. I dashed to get it, hoping it was Kim or Kendrick, but it was neither. It was a call from a job I applied for.

"Yes, this is Candi Mathews. 2:30? Yes, that works great for me. See you then," I ended the conversation.

"Who was that? Your lil boyfriend?" Greg said with sarcasm.

"No, a job interview. I may be moving to Atlanta if it works out," I said with confidence.

"You should hook me up with your friend, JRock, so we can do double dates with you and Daisy. I'm sure he can show me around," I said, hoping it would throw him off the thought of me hooking up with him.

"I'll try to do that. But what will I get out of the deal if I do? I need you to do somethin' for me, Candi." He put his arm around my waist and pulled me toward him. He put his tongue in my ear and whispered, "You know you can stay here as long as you need to. I'll take care of you if you take care of me."

I heard Kim honk the horn. Startled, we pulled away from one another. I didn't respond to Greg's deceptive offer. I quickly grabbed the rental keys and my purse off the counter, and I headed for the door. As I approached Kim's car, my mind swirled on what just happened. I wondered if Daisy knew who she was really married to. I was ashamed of myself for feeling a little tempted to take him up on his offer. His advances did kind of turn me on. I hadn't had real dick in months. Kendrick only liked head while I had to get myself off with a dildo. Some in-house dick would be good. Daisy and I weren't real cousins anyway. Our moms were just really close friends, and we grew up next door to each other. Hell, her boujee ass might be on some threesome shit anyway.

"Hey girl," Kim yelled.

"I'll follow you," I replied.

I drove behind Kim for about thirty minutes before I saw the airport signs. When we got off the exit, I pulled into the rental drop-off section while Kim parked and waited for me.

When I got in the car with Kim, she was on the phone. I heard her say that she had an appointment at 2:00 pm. Damn. So much for a ride to the interview, but I put it out there anyway.

"Hey, is there any way you can take me to your friend's office for an interview at 2:30 today?" I asked.

"You're in luck because that was her on the phone. I have to go drop somethin' off to her at 2:00. So, we can hang out till then."

"You're a lifesaver, Kim. Thank you so much."

As we pulled out into the airport traffic, I gazed out of the window at all the people coming and going out of *Hartsfield*. Among the crowd, I saw Kendrick going into the airport. It looked like he and another woman were about to catch a flight. I told Kim to stop the car before jumping out and running into the airport. I didn't have time to explain to Kim what I was doing. By the time I reached the entryway, Kendrick was out of sight. My phone buzzed inside my pocket. It was Kim. I checked the text.

Kim: WTF? Where are you?

I texted back, *sorry, thought I saw someone I knew. I'm coming back out of N5.*

As soon as I entered the car, Kim went in on me, but I wasn't in the mood to discuss it with her.

"Damn trick, I thought you saw President Obama, the way you hopped out of this car!" Kim yelled out.

"No, I thought I saw an old friend from back home," I lied.

We rode in silence for a few minutes. I wondered where Kendrick was going, and who was that girl? Why hadn't he tried to contact me? He knew my number. He was one of the few people left in the world who remembered phone numbers, so I knew damn well he hadn't forgotten mine. As much as he dialed it from prison, it should be programmed in his brain. I missed our phone sex. Hell, I missed our in-person sex, too. I loved the way he looked at me when I let him cum in my mouth. I loved him so much, and I'd do anything for us to be together. I hope he hadn't gotten back to Atlanta and forgotten about me. I really thought we had something special. Come to think of it, he was probably flying out to Texas to see me. I shouldn't have tried to surprise him and just told him I was staying in Atlanta to find us somewhere to live. My dad said he would pay for a place, but I had to find a job first to prove that I was serious.

"Fuck!" I shouted.

Kim hit the brakes hard and sent us both flying toward the dashboard. "What is it now, girl?" she shouted.

"I can't go to the interview like this. I have on these damn jeans and sneakers."

"No problem. I have to swing by my house to pick up what I need to take to Sophia anyway. I probably have something you can wear."

We pulled up to Kim's house a half-hour later. I began to see that Atlanta was small, and every destination took at least a half-hour to get to. Kim's house was beautiful. It was laid from the front door to the back. You would never think she had kids because it was spotless. She went upstairs and returned a few minutes later with business suits.

"I know you're a size 8, so I have a few new things you can have."

"Thank you. Because I didn't bring any business attire with me," I responded.

"No problem, girl. Any cousin of Daisy's is a cousin to me. You're family. Go ahead. You can use the guest bathroom in my office down the hall. It's a full bath."

I walked down the hall and admired the detail in the crown molding. The bathroom was plush too. Kim and Daisy were living like some Real Atlanta Housewives. I desired to have something like this for Kendrick and me.

I changed my clothes. The suit fitted me well, and I looked great in it. I never bought nice quality clothes. My mom always told me that I needed to, but I chose to keep my nigga fresh rather than me. I loved to see a good-looking man. But now that I was in Atlanta, I needed to step my game up.

Kim and I arrived at Sophia Patton's Realty at 1:59. She went in first to handle whatever business she had with Mrs. Patton, then I went in. She asked me a few basic questions before asking if I could start tomorrow.

"Yes. Absolutely," I replied.

"Are you willing to stay on the property? I have to ask because it's a tax credit apartment complex, and you may encounter tenants. Some managers like to interact with tenants, and some don't."

Look at God. I wanted to say *hell yeah*, but I politely said, " Yes, that's not a problem."

She handed me the keys to an apartment, gave me the address to the property, and told me to ask for Caren when I made it to the office.

"She will fill you in on your duties over there."

"Thank you."

She quickly stated, "Oh, don't thank me, honey. You were highly recommended by Kim. Thank her," she winked and smiled.

When Kim and I drove to the property, to my surprise, it was a lovely apartment complex. Village at Carver. It had a nice ring to it. It was close to downtown Atlanta and close to Marta, so I could definitely make it work for Kendrick and me until something better came along.

Thank God, the apartment was fully furnished. It was used as a model home for open houses, so I didn't have to buy new furniture. But I would lie to my dad and tell him I needed it, so I'd have spending money for Kendrick and me. Kim said she had to be somewhere and asked if I was good with staying there. "Girl, yes. I'm at home now," I said as we laughed. She dropped me off at the management office in front of the complex.

"I'll hit you later to make sure you're straight."

"Okay. And oh, Kim. Thank you so much for everything."

I walked into the office and asked for Caren. She was a white lady with stringy blonde hair. It looked like she bleached it daily because it was fried. She showed me my office and gave me a rundown of how things worked.

After the benediction, Caren said, "Welcome aboard."

"Glad to be here. I look forward to working with you," I replied, shaking her hand.

I walked to my new apartment with a smile on my face. As I walked, I heard a familiar voice in the distance. It was coming from a group of guys standing near one of the buildings. When I got closer, I saw that it was TMax, Kendrick's friend.

"Hey TMax, how are you?" I said, walking toward him. The guys stopped their conversation and looked at me. TMax stepped toward me, standing in a defensive pose.

"Who you, and how you know me?"

Confused, I replied, "I'm Kendrick's friend from Texas, remember? We rode..." he interrupted me.

"Hold up, lil lady. If you lookin' for him, he ain't around here. Don't be walkin' up on me asking all kinds of questions about people." His large stature towered over me.

I was pretty intimidated and embarrassed, to say the least, but I needed to get to my man, and TMax was my only hope. I stood my ground.

"No, I'm not looking for him at this moment. I just wanted to let y'all know I work here at the management office now. Also, I'm staying in apartment 8A. If and when you do see him, tell him to holler at me. Please."

"Bet, I'll do that, lil lady. But I need you to let me finish this crap game, Aight?"

"Aight cool. No problem."

I walked away from TMax with my head still high and my spirits even greater. Today was a good day. I almost sang it in my Ice Cube voice as I strutted home, elated about my new apartment. God was really showing me favor in the ATL

Chapter Twelve: Trouble

I called Trey and JRock to let them know that I was back with the product. We agreed to meet at our usual spot. I dropped my driver off and headed to my loft to shower and change clothes. I couldn't wait to get off this work to put some money into this new artist I'm managing. The little dude had bars, and his sound was lit, so I knew he could blow up overnight with the right strategy.

The boys and I met at one of the vacant apartments at Carver Homes. The white chick, Caren, in the leasing office allowed us to do our business there in exchange for money. Trey fucked with her on the powder. Her ass even pranced around the complex, looking for some black dick, and Trey gave it to her every chance he could. She was cool enough to let us know when the police were on the property. I didn't know how Trey maneuvered around his baby mama because she lived there too. Shit got wild sometimes, though, because his baby mama is hood as hell. She would beat a bitch ass about Trey, and she would go toe to toe with his big ass too when he got too far out-of-pocket.

As I drove up, I saw Trey walking to the apartment and JRock pulling up behind me. These niggas were on time for the money, but any other time they were late as hell. We all dapped it up and made it inside.

"Nigga, that SS clean as hell. When did you get it out the paint shop," I asked Trey.

"Man, I picked it up yesterday. That bitch hittin', ain't it?" He grinned.

"Hell yeah. But it ain't gettin' no bitches like that G Wagon," JRock butted in.

"Da fuck you mean? I get the pussy I need to get, and that's all that matter, nigga," Trey said in his defense. We laughed at the thought of his big ass getting pussy.

After we counted up the money we made for the week, we squared up on the distribution, and parlayed about the big New Year's Eve party coming up. The radio stations were having all kinds of hot shit going on to bring in the new year. This year V103 was hosting an All-White Old School party at The Velvet Room downtown. One of our homeboys managed it, so we were already in that bitch. Everybody and their mama was going to be there. All the movers and shakers would be there for sure. If a nigga ain't getting no money, this was not the event to be. Niggas were going to be bossed up like a muthafucka. I couldn't wait for me and my baby, Kim, to hit the scene. I just copped a white Maserati Ghibli that I hadn't yet told anybody about, so we would be bringing in the new year riding hard too.

I hit Kim up to check on her. She was out of school for Christmas break, but she'd been working hard at the tax office getting ready for the upcoming tax season. However, we had to get our Christmas shopping done for her kids and my daughter. She was big on family, and I loved that about her.

I stepped out and called her. She picked up on the second ring.

"Hey, love, how are you?"

"I'm good, babe. I miss you. Where are you?" I asked.

"I'm shutting down the office, but I can be wherever you need me to be."

Damn, her voice was so sexy. She made my dick get hard just thinking about her. This girl was definitely trouble. My mama told me one day that I was going to meet my match--somebody who was going to tame my womanizing ass down. Kim was just like my mama in so many ways. She didn't know that I was peeping her playa game. She had a nigga for everything. Her contact list was on fire. If her car needed fixing, she knew a guy. If her plumbing burst, she knew a guy. If she needed a lawyer.... guess what? She had a nigga on speed dial. My mama did the same shit. She loved my daddy. He was a womanizer like me, but if he couldn't take care of something around the house, she always had someone else who could. I'd learned everything about a woman from my mama. That's how I knew women knew how to run the game better than a man. That's why I kept a few on my team. Trey and JRock told me that they didn't know how my ass pulled all these high-class women, but my gift of gab was impeccable. It could pass every test known to man. Plus, most uppity women were weakened by a good dick game. They tried to play hard, and I let them, but after they get the dick, they fall in love. Then I dropped their ass like a hot potato if it ain't about the money. In my book, stupid is, as stupid does. I didn't love these hoes, and I surely didn't need one who couldn't help advance me or keep up when I'm on the come up.

Kim wasn't like that. She was intelligent, attractive, and for some reason, good dick didn't faze her at all. We vibed on a *building empire* level. She had me intrigued like a muthafucka. I planned to enjoy watching her fall in love with me. After she figured out that she didn't need anyone but me, she would fall. I realized that she had been through bullshit in her life. She didn't trust niggas further than what she could get out of them, but I promised myself that I would change that. Kim was soulmate material. Her mind is rare, like a precious diamond. You don't find too many with what I call a triple threat. She got book sense, street sense, and common sense. I've been searching for her my whole life.

"Do you want me to pick you up, so we can go Christmas shopping?" I asked.

"You can if you're nearby. I'll leave my car here because I need to be back in the morning, anyway."

"Bet. I'm on the way. But hey, I need a good date for the people to come by to professionally decorate your tree. Check your calendar and let me know when I get there," I said before hanging up.

Before I headed to the car, Trey stopped me. "Hold up, man. I knew I forgot to tell you somethin'. Yo girl from Texas workin' up at the rental office. She's stayin' up there in 8A. She's our new landlord, bruh." He burst out laughing while talking.

"What the fuck you mean?" I palmed my face in disgust. This was news that I didn't want to hear.

"That crazy girl from Texas didn't go back to Texas, bruh. I saw her walkin' through here the other day, and she recognized me. Scared the shit out of me too. I thought she was the police, but Caren told me she just hired her as an assistant as a favor for a mutual friend they have. You might need to handle that because she is a wild card, playa," He insisted.

"Bet, bruh. Say less." We dapped, and I drove off.

How the fuck did this bitch know where I be posted? She must've been on some stalking-type shit. I couldn't deal with this shit today. But I knew that I had to get at her soon because she was terrible for all my damn business. How the fuck did I deserve this nonsense? Dumb hoes can be so unpredictable.

Chapter Thirteen: Too Much Info

Keith and I had so much fun during the Christmas holiday. We went all out with the kids, and it went well. Everybody was happy. Tonight, we were going out to dinner, just the two of us. The twins were with my mom because Tanya was still M.I.A. I was even more worried about her. I hadn't heard from her in nearly two months. To top it off, I was so emotional for some reason and my mind was all over the place.

We pulled into the Fogo de Chao parking lot and allowed the valet to park the car. The host seated us in a quiet little corner. I'm glad because I wanted to mention the conversation I had with Calvin to Keith in private.

Once we were seated, I jumped into the conversation. "Babe, I want to thank you again for a wonderful Christmas. You made me and the girls so happy."

"You don't have to thank me, babe. It's my job as a man to make sure you are happy. You never have to worry when you are with me. I got you. I'll do anything to keep that beautiful smile on your face."

"The twins' dad said to thank you, too," I blurted out.

"Oh really? You talk to him about me? You must like me a lot." He laughed.

"Don't flatter yourself. I try to run people by him when they're around our kids," I shut his arrogance down.

"Oh, so I got to interview with this nigga?" He said, bewildered. I couldn't read his expression, and it was making me uncomfortable. I wanted this to be a pleasant night where we ended it with laughter. Eager to finish, I repositioned myself in the chair and sat up straight.

"No, not at all. Actually, he knows you. He says y'all were locked up together," I continued to observe his face.

"Oh, yeah? Where he down at?" He said without giving any cues.

I learned that when a nigga had been down the road and done some foul shit in prison, he didn't want anyone from the inside talking about it on the outside. There were a lot of niggas that came home on that down-low shit and didn't want anyone to know about what they did in prison. They'd go back to their ladies and ask them to do weird shit, like play in their assholes. Some girls ignored the signs just to keep a nigga. When I see suspect shit, I take heed. Hell, for all I know, Calvin could've been covering up that shit because he was loyal like that. But either way, I'm about to find out what the hell Keith is up to.

"Coffee County. He says you owe him money for some chess games, but I told him that I be whooping your ass in chess, so y'all even. His name is Calvin Collins."

Keith almost spat out his drink, coughing and clearing his throat.

"Are you okay?" I leaned over and patted his back.

"Hold up. Calvin Collins is your ex? That's my nigga! This can't be happening," he shook his head in disgust. "I can't be with my nigga's girl." He backed up his chair like he was about to leave.

"No, No, No, calm down. It's not what you think. He is the twins' dad, but we have never been together."

"What the fuck you mean, y'all ain't been together? How the hell did you have two kids by the man then? I wish you would have told me earlier. I would have backed off, Shawty. This is messed up for real. I do business and have mad respect for that dude. He is like a brother to me."

I started laughing. "Will you calm down? You're making a scene."

"Ain't shit funny about this, Kim, and a scene is the least of my worries. I don't play these types of games with hoes. My loyalty goes beyond these streets."

Now, I am upset. Here I was trying to tell this man something good, and he was screaming to me about some stupid nigga loyalty code he'd made.

"Why? You think he's going to tell me something bad about you? He didn't! He spoke highly of you. But who the fuck you calling a hoe?" I blurted out.

"No, I just don't like when bitches be puttin' niggas against each other on BS. I should have done better homework on this situation before..."

I wanted to know where Keith's anger was coming from. I'd never seen this side of him. I didn't like it, but I wasn't going to be another bitch or hoe to him. I shut his ass down.

"Before what? Look nigga, I didn't birth the twins. My best friend Tashia did. She and Calvin were a couple. If you remember, I told you she was killed in a drive-by shooting."

"Yeah, but..." he started.

"Yeah, but nothing. This might be too much information, but she was pregnant with the twins at the time. They survived. Calvin and I are raisin' them together. End of story. You can take that however you want, but I'm leaving." I stood up to leave. Despite my rage, I left him with one last piece of my mind. "You got me twisted if you think I'm on some foul shit! Fuck you and fuck all that shit you standin' on. Just remember, I wanted you. I don't fuckin' need you. Goodbye, Mr. Thomas," I shouted as I stomped out of the restaurant.

"Kim. Kim, I'm sorry. Wait," Keith said, running behind me.

By the time he paid the ticket and came outside, I was in an Uber pulling off. I couldn't believe that this nigga tried me on some hoe shit after I had closed down everything and everybody for his ass. I'd missed out on plenty of money while l was laid up with Keith. Guys were so stupid. He was going to break up with me just because of who he *thought* Calvin was to me. I would never understand these street nigga codes, but what I did know was that I didn't have time for immature little boys who had pissing contests. I was out.

My phone rang inside of my purse. I checked the notification. It was Keith. I sent him to voicemail three times back-to-back and ignored his text messages. When I got home, I relaxed in my steamy shower, threw on my pajamas, and drank a glass of wine. I checked my phone. Keith called four more times and texted six. Jaylen also texted. *WYD?*

I let out a deep sigh. Fuck it. Keith wanted hoe shit. I'd give him hoe shit. There was money to be made. I texted Jaylen back and asked, *"Where you at......"*

Chapter Fourteen: Time Limit

Damn, I didn't mean to go off on Kim like that, but she blew my mind with that information about Calvin. I remembered him mentioning that he had twins. I saw a few pictures of them on his wall, but I never looked at them. When you're in jail, niggas didn't eyeball pictures of other nigga's children. Somebody might think you're jacking off to their kid and kill you, especially if you were in there for child molestation. Not that I was, but I didn't want to get caught in nothing of that kind either. I stayed in my lane while I was down. Calvin was a cool nigga. We became good friends. He saved my life, while I was locked up and I'll never forget it. One time a female CO tried me up on some bullshit. That shit went left out of nowhere.

Calvin and I orchestrated a whole hustling operation in our dorm. JRock and Trey would supply us with weed, cocaine, cigarettes, cell phones, or whatever we needed. They would send it through some broads who would give the items to the inmates on work details or the female CO's we had on our team. I was fucking this one CO bitch, and I guess I was laying the pipe too good because she caught feelings and tried to set my ass up because she saw that my baby mama came to visit me. Calvin caught wind of her plan from another CO and told me about it. We moved our shit around, and when she brought the dogs into my cell to shake me down, I didn't have anything. But her ass still threw my ass in solitary for about six months.

I stopped fucking with her ass altogether, and shit got worse. She had the folks watching me so close, I couldn't maneuver. She stopped all my visitation and wall phone privileges. I had a cell phone but that bitch had eyes on my every move so I couldn't bring it out on any of the shifts. Most inmates don't like when a nigga make the dorm hot, so I had to just chill. Calvin held it down for me and didn't short any of the money. He had my back, and he was as solid as they come. On another occasion, the same bitter ass hoe sent some little gang niggas at me on the yard, and they tried to run up on me with that gangsta shit. That was until Calvin, and a few of our crew came rushing in. We stomped one of them lil niggas to sleep, and his ass never woke up. She tried to hit me with a free world charge. Calvin got his lawyer to make a few calls, and I beat that shit and got her ass fired. That nigga Calvin always came through. He had a lot of pull in and out of the joint. I like how he moved. I'll never forget how solid he was and still is. We are still doing business. He made sure that we both ate on the inside. After I got out, I made sure he could still eat. For that loyalty, I pay homage to Bruh with everything I touch. I break bread with him on everything I do in the streets, so he could handle his appeal and survive in that bitch. He taught me to look at the game from a different angle and take my hustling to the next level. I would never betray him, especially with a female.

Never in a million years would I have thought that I would be with the woman raising his kids. This shit was getting crazier by the day. I began to believe that my karma was coming back to bite my ass between this and Candi. But fuck that, I needed to talk to Kim and apologize. But she was acting like one of these dumb broads she claimed that she wasn't. If she didn't get at me by New Year's Eve, I was going to the party without her and move on. There were plenty of bitches that wanted to be down with me. It was probably best I leave her alone anyway. Starting now, I put Kim on a time limit. I needed to clear my head. All these women's BS had me exhausted. Maybe a night out with my boys would cheer me up and get my mind off her. Shiid, I hadn't hit the strip club with them in a minute. I'd hit their ass and put together a nigga turn-up night.

I hit JRock's phone first, but he didn't pick up. I then called Trey. JRock's ass was probably somewhere tricking off. Trey picked up. I heard kids in the background.

"What up, Bruh? What you gettin' into tonight," I asked.

"Oh shiid, I ain't doin' shit. My ol' lady went out with her sister them and got me babysittin'," He replied. He sounded depressed, like his baby mama had sentenced him to death or something.

"Nigga parents don't babysit. You the pappy, Bruh. You're just at home takin' care of your family, Bruh," I said. We both laughed.

"Whatever, Bruh. If that's the case, they mama need to hurry her ass back because these kids 'bout to drive me crazy. I done dozed off on they ass twice already, but Junior ain't goin' for it. He is all over me. But it's cool, though. You know they are my everythin'," Trey admitted.

"Yeah, man, I know what you mean. My daughter is the same way. I wish I could see her more, but my crazy baby mama be trippin'. You know her crazy ass sent the stuff back that I sent my daughter for Christmas? I spent hella money on clothes, shoes, electronics, and money orders worth five bands, and she sent it all back."

"Oh, word? Bruh, that's fucked up."

"Yeah, she still bitter because I left her ass. When I was in prison, she came to visit me and told me that if I wasn't going to be with her, I wouldn't see my child again. She wasn't playing either. I haven't seen my kid since I got out.

I been callin', but she hangs up soon as she hears my voice. I send money every month, but she sends it back every time. Shit crazy, man."

"Damn dog. I didn't know it was like that."

"Yeah. So nigga, cherish that shit you got goin'. Havin' yo kids under the same roof as you is a blessing. You feel me?"

"Yeah. I feel ya, bruh. What yo ass up to tonight? Sounds like you lost your best friend. You need a shoulder to cry on or somethin'," Trey joked.

"Nigga, hell nawl! Fuck these hoes. I'm tryin' to hit the strip club tonight, but I see your ass playin' daddy daycare and shit," I replied, trying to sound hard. This shit with Kim was bothering the fuck out of me though. The scene at the restaurant was still running laps in my head. She had helped me pick out different gifts for my daughter. It felt like we were becoming a blended family, but here we are back at square one.

"Oh shiid, boi. My girl will be back before midnight. She knows she can't stay out past that. So, I can meet you there. Which one you hittin', Gold Rush?" he inquired.

"Hell yeah. Say less, Bruh. See you there," I replied. Before he hangs up, I can hear him hollering at the kids to get down off of something. I laughed to myself. Those kids were giving his ass hell over there.

I headed to my loft in Buckhead to get ready. I wore black Versace from head to toe. Grabbing the keys to my black Range Rover, I head out. Before I pulled off, I found Jeezy's song *All Black Everything* on Apple Music. I hit 85 South towards the Atlanta skyline nodding to the beat. You never knew what a night like this would bring, but I was ready for whatever.

I stopped at Tower Package Store on Pryor Street and grabbed a bottle of Hennessy, a cup of ice, Red Bull, and blunts. While standing at my car door, busting a swisher sweet, I heard someone call my government name. It sounded like the police. I stood still for a moment and prepared myself for some bullshit.

"Keith Thomas! Little Keith Thomas. Is that you, boy? Damn boy, you look like one of those rappers," a voice shouted.

I slowly turned around to see a tattered old man with gray hair standing at the front of my car. I could hardly recognize him. It was my middle school principal Mr. Shepard. He and I used to get into it during my manhood transition. He caught me selling candy, CDs, or whatever I was hustling at the time and dragged me into his office for long lectures about how I was going down the wrong path. He even talked my mama into letting him be my mentor to help deter my mischievous ways. I admired him for giving me his time and effort. I never disrespected him like Trey and JRock did. When we found out Mr. Shepard was smoking dope, it broke my heart, but them two niggas used to dog him out. He was an intelligent man, and he cared deeply about the underprivileged communities of Atlanta. Especially the kids.

"How are you doin', Mr. Shepard? I haven't seen you around here in a long time".

"Yeah, Thomas. I had to slow it down. This old mind can't keep up with y'all youngsters anymore. It sure is good to see you doing good for yourself, Thomas. You were always the smart one. I've always wanted to thank you for the respect you've shown me over the years. I was really down, but you never changed your respect for me. I'll always be grateful for that."

"Mr. Shepard, you don't owe me that. If anything, I owe you. You were there for me when my dad wasn't. It'll always be love and respect with me and you. You showed me the other side of life. You taught me that there was a whole world out there, and my mind didn't have to be confined to just these streets."

"Thank you, young man. Thank you for saying that. I tried to give all you guys a way out of here. It's more to life than money and what y'all call it Bling, Bling." We laughed aloud at the outdated reference.

"Have you gotten married yet, Thomas?"

"No, sir. I'm still out here chasing these women. You know it's hard to find a good one."

"It's hard because you're chasing, son. God will put the perfect woman in your path to stop you from doing all that running. She'll find you soon.

I laughed at that because I wasn't thinking about marrying anybody. Mr. Shepard had always been longwinded, but he never got on my nerves. As I got older, I realized the importance of his speeches. I could listen to him all day. He was actually the one who taught me to speak Spanish.

"Yeah, she is definitely going to have to find me because I ain't trying to find her, " I replied. I threw my hand up and shook my head as if marriage would be the end of the world and gave a farewell to Mr. Shepard.

I glanced at the backseat through my rearview mirror. Kim's gift was still sitting there. I bought her a pair of diamond stud earrings. She had been wanting some for a while. I made it a custom to get her something each time we went out, but she stormed out of the restaurant so fast, I didn't have the chance to give her a gift this time. I decided to call her again. I knew she was mad, but damn, she had to understand that was some heavy shit she laid on me. Of course, she wasn't going to answer. I let the phone ring until it went to voicemail. I texted to apologize for the sixth time. I was sorry that I hurt her feelings, but she was acting like a damn child by not picking up her phone. I wasn't going to put any more energy into her tonight though. Fuck it, I'm about to have a good time with my niggas. I lit my blunt and took a sip of that Hen dog and headed to the club. I texted Trey and JRock, while in route.

To Trey: Almost at the spot. Hit me when you OTW.

To JRock: Yo, we headed to the strip club. Come thru.

To Kash: Come through Gold Rush when you're done performing.

***

The club was packed with cars everywhere. I paid three hundred dollars to park near the entrance. You never knew what could happen in the club, so I needed easy access to my whip and my 9mm. I saw one of my homeboys working security, so I tucked my piece in the small of my back under my shirt. While he performed the routine search on me, I asked him why they were so packed tonight. He mentioned that some radio station's DJ was debuting new artists tonight.

"Oh, okay, that's what's up," I responded. He tapped my back and gave me a look to signal that I couldn't take my gun in. I slid him five hundred to let me keep it on me. He gave me a nod, and I walked in the entrance, strapped.

I paid my entrance and VIP fee, which came with two bottles. I didn't have time to be standing around. Although there were music industry people in there, there were some street wolves here too. I was already tipsy from the Loud and Hennessey, so I needed a seat with a view. I didn't want any bad vibes tonight, so whoever came around me tonight was going to have a good time too. The hostess walked me to my VIP section. I saw different types of niggas and females in there. As soon as I sat down, two average looking dancers walked up and asked if I wanted a dance.

"Not right now, sweetie, but I'll get at you later," I responded.

"Okay, baby. Don't forget me now," the thick one said.

She licked her lips and grabbed my wrist with her bear claws, holding on for dear life. I thought of the scene in *The Players Club* when Dollar Bill hit the sirens and said, "Money. Money. Money". The chicks in here are on a paper chase tonight, and I didn't blame them. I came to drop a few stacks and that wasn't something I usually did.

" I got you, sweetie. Come back around my table later," I instructed.

"Okay, boo," she said with a big Colgate smile. Chicks think they got all the game.

I poured a drink and observed my surroundings. I had a great view of the whole club. When you were getting the kind of money we were getting in these streets, you had to expect the unexpected. I didn't need a nigga or his crew getting any ideas on pulling a whack-ass robbery. You never knew who was out here in the streets catching feelings about your paper. A hater was always lurking.

My phone buzzed. I whisked it out of my pocket, hoping it was Kim, but it was Trey. The music was so loud I could hardly hear him. He told me that he was on his way and that he was bringing a few little niggas from the block with him.

By that time, my food had come, so I sat back, nibbled on my wings, and enjoyed the scene. My mouth dropped as I noticed this fine-ass redbone coming out from the back. She looked like an angel in her all-white sheer outfit. The central air flowed through her dress as she walked. She made her rounds, thanking each dude who tipped her while she performed. I'd come here so much that I was familiar with the dancers' routine. She noticed me staring at her before coming toward my section. I knew that she wanted to see what the new money was looking like.

"Would you like a dance, sexy?" she asked. We locked eyes. Everything about her was perfect.

"Sure, why not. How much are they, " I asked, although I already knew the price. Me and fellas come in here all the time.

"Twenty dollars for a table dance, baby," She replied. I placed five hundred in her garter.

"In that case, I need twenty-five dances," I replied. I saw her eyes widen in delight. She knew that she had hit the jackpot. Game recognizes game, and money is the universal game changer.

I sat back and let her do her thang. Strippers cut the small talk and danced when they were getting paid. When they weren't making any money, they wanted to sit in your face and make conversation. I wasn't a fan of that stripper talk. They were slick, begging for business, but if a nigga was going to fuck with you, he was going to fuck with you. There were very few men coming in here just for conversation. So, she wouldn't have to do all that seductive gibberish. However, a man was only going to pay for what he was willing to fuck. If you didn't turn him on, he was not giving you shit, no matter how long you sat or shook your ass in his face.

After about ten songs, Trey and two young cats arrived. I told ol' girl to take a break, change her clothes, and bring some more girls back with her.

I dapped it up with Trey and the little homies. Their eyes were wide open, ready for action. They reminded me of us when we were younger. Trey's uncle had us in all the strip clubs and traps before we reached puberty. I told them to have a seat and help themselves with the drinks and food. "It's on me tonight, Fellas."

"Oh, word? In that case, I want her and her," I heard one of them say as I walked off to the cash station.

I gave the attendee five bands. She put it through the money counter and counterfeit tester. Then she handed me forty-five hundred in one dollar bills.

"Have a nice night, handsome," she said.

"Thank you. I'm goin' to do my best," I replied.

I stopped by the DJ booth to make a request. It wasn't the usual DJ I knew. Of course, it was some industry cat, who had been paid to work the party. He shot me down and said he didn't make requests. I slid him five hundred and handed him my artist, Kash's mixtape. Everything was for sale, so I knew he would do what I needed him to do. I'm glad I told Kash to come through. What better way to get your shit heard than in front of the whole radio industry?

When I made it back to VIP, everybody had ass in their face. I put the money on the table and took my seat. Redbone came back in a diamond-chain type outfit. Her titties and ass were hanging out just how I liked. When the light hit the diamonds, they sparkled, illuminating throughout the club. She did *not* come to play. Baby girl was putting on just like me. I gave her a wink and a nod to let her know she did good. I liked what she was offering. When Kash's song *Fire* started to play, the club got lit. With drinks in the air, everybody chanted, "We got that fire". Redbone posted up between my legs, swaying her hips to the beat. Oh yeah, this was about to be a good night.

After partying with several girls throughout the night, everything was good, or so I thought. I stood up, the Hennessy had kicked all the way in. I was so lit, I could barely walk. I looked over at Trey. That nigga was having the time of his life. He had bad bitches all over him.

"Hey, nigga I'm goin' to the bathroom," I hollered over the music.

"Okay, Bruh. I'm 'bout to take this baddie into the VIP room." He placed his hand on my shoulders and whispered, "I'm tryin' to cut with this bitch, bruh." We laughed.

" You wild, bruh. You wild. But hey, have fun and scrap up, Nigga."

As I turned the corner to the bathroom, I saw Redbone talking to a guy. Just as I was about to pass them, the dude bumped my shoulder. He pushed up off me like he wanted some smoke.

"Watch where you goin' drunk ass nigga," he said, puffing up his chest.

He stood in front of two of his boys as if he was trying to impress them. I stood my ground and stared at him dead in his eyes.

"Hey, bruh, who the fuck you talking to? You better keep that shit movin'. This ain't what you want." He started to walk up on me, but I raised my shirt, showing off my piece.

"Nigga, ain't shit drunk about me or this nine. What's up?"

He backed up and said some shit like he would catch me later, but I walked away towards the bathroom. I knew he didn't want to die in a damn strip club.

I stood in front of the urinal and pissed for what felt like ten minutes. I closed my eyes and leaned back and forth a couple of times. When I opened them, the room was fucking empty. Even the restroom attendant was gone. What the fuck? I heard a loud ringing in my ear. Falling to the ground, I blacked out for a second. When I gained consciousness, three niggas were kicking and stomping my head and torso.

I heard one say, "Use your piece now, punk-ass nigga." I tried to tuck and roll, but they were kicking me every way I turned on the floor. My gun slid across the floor and was now out of reach, but I had enough strength to make a leap for it. In midair, I heard the door open. It was Trey, the two lil homies, and Kash. They busted in that muthafucka like Rambo. Trey had guns in both hands with silencers on each. "I know we don't have a problem here, gentlemen. K, you aight bruh," Trey asked.

"Yeah, dawg, I'm good," I replied as one of the lil homies gave me his hand and pulled me off the floor.

"Come on, big homie. We gotcha."

I walked over to Trey, took the gun out of his hand, and pointed it at the big tough nigga who brought all this unnecessary attention.

I walked closer and placed the gun on his left temple. He pleaded with me to spare his life.

"Oh, nigga you didn't want to hear me earlier when I said to keep that shit movin'. Now you want me to listen to you. Nigga, fuck you! I bet you hear me now," I said. Then, I pulled the trigger. His left ear went flying in the air in a million pieces. He screamed so loud and grabbed the left side of his head. Blood leaked through his fingers onto his shoulder and onto the floor as he dropped to his knees. The other two niggas tried to move toward him, but Trey and the homies had their ass frozen in time. As we backed out of the bathroom, passing the threshold, I reached in my pocket and gave the bathroom attendant a stack of ones.

"Since you let these punk-ass niggas in here on me, you can show me another way out of here from back here. And I know you ain't seen shit, right?" I directed. He nodded, pointing to a closed-off hallway that led to an exit door. We hauled ass to the car. I jumped in the car with Trey and tossed my keys to the lil homies, telling them to follow us. I told Kash to get the hell out of dodge. He didn't need any of this type of heat right now. He agreed and went the opposite way.

"Man, Trey, good lookin' out, bruh. Them niggas had my ass down bad."

"Bruh, we family. I gotcha back because you always got mine. I was headed to the VIP when that red ass chick stopped and told me you might be in trouble. Nigga, you knew I was on the way to see them niggas the long way," Trey bragged. He held his gun up and laughed. I chuckled. I'm glad his instincts stayed on point because my ass would have been fucked up.

We pulled up in front of Trey's crib in Carver homes, and the lil homies pulled up right behind us. We stood outside and kicked shit for about thirty minutes, laughing about the crazy night. I gave the lil homies their props for stepping up and handling business, thanking them for being there for me. I assured them that they had earned their place on our team. I knew they were excited, but they both held their composure and dapped me up like real goons do. I jumped in my truck and rolled down the window.

"Yo, I'll holla at y'all ass tomorrow. I'm takin' my ass home. Y'all hold it down."

"Bet, my nigga. Luv you, bruh," Trey replied

"Luv, you too, bruh."

As I turned the corner to leave the complex, I saw a sign that said *Bldg. A 1-8* with an arrow pointing left. I thought about Candi. This night couldn't get any worse, so I might as well face the music with her ass.

Chapter Fifteen: A Woman's Touch

I got out and knocked on her door three times. She answered without even asking who it was. When she saw it was me, she fell into my arms and started kissing me.

"Kendrick! What happened to you? Where have you been? I missed you so much," she said as I limped over to the couch. There was something about being around a woman's touch that made your pain seem less painful.

"I'm good, just had a little run-in at the club. What's up with you, though?" I asked.

She walked to the kitchen, put some ice in a dishtowel, and placed it on my head.

"I've been working and waiting on you to come to see me. I knew TMax would tell you." That was her reply. I swear women think they got all the sense. She knew damn well what I meant.

"No, I mean, why are you *here*? You're supposed to be in Texas," I asked again, with clarification.

"Let's not talk about that right now, baby. You're hurt. Let me take care of you," she replied. I must admit, the ice pack did feel good. A woman's touch always made a hurt nigga feel good, but I needed to know what the fuck she was up to. Well, maybe it can wait, because she started taking my clothes off to inspect my injuries. She unzipped my pants and asked me to stand up. When I did, she slid my pants down to my ankles. I didn't know if it was the Hennessy or weed that had me horny as fuck right now, but damn if, Candi ain't giving me life. She knelt down and began sucking my dick. It didn't feel great, but it would do. After I nut in her mouth, I told her to go take a shower, so we could get in the bed. She tried to resist, telling me that she took a shower earlier, but I told her that we could take one together. Sadly, I had to trick her into bathing. However, it's the only way that I was fucking her.

After showering and getting in bed, I fucked Candi to sleep. I laid next to her, thinking about Kim. I got my phone and texted her: *Baby, I'm so sorry. Please meet me for lunch tomorrow, so we can talk about it, please.*

I rolled over, turned my back to Candi, and drifted off to sleep.

Chapter Sixteen: The Audacity

Jaylen was outside of his house when I pulled up. I saw him putting something in his trunk. I sat in my car and waited for him to ask me to get out. To be honest, I didn't want to be here. I didn't know why I was here either. As he walked upon the passenger side, I rolled down my window.

"Hey, beautiful. You hungry? Let's go get somethin' to eat," He asked.

"Sure. You want me to drive my car and meet you somewhere?" I asked.

"No, I'm goin' to ride with you," He replied.

He had never ridden with me anywhere. I wasn't in the mood for a date, especially with his ass. I just wanted to get my mind off of Keith and make some money while doing it. However, I had driven all the way over to Jaylen's, and I didn't want to leave empty-handed by turning down his little fake date. So, I gave in.

"Okay, cool. Hop in."

He got in and I put my car in reverse and drove off.

"Where to?" I asked.

"I got a taste for some wings. Let's go to the lil strip club up the street. They have good food," he instructed.

"Which one, Pleasers or Gold Rush," I asked.

He started laughing and said, "Girl, you know you don't be in the hood. Pleasers been closed. He then looked at me intently and said, " Let's do Gold Rush".

" Hell, I don't know. I don't go to strip clubs on the regular, but okay, cool. I need to get gas first, though," I responded.

We hopped on Lee Street from the West End then hit Sylvan Road. I stopped at the Shell gas station on Cleveland Avenue. As soon as I parked in front of the pump, I got out to pay for the gas. As Jaylen pumped the gas, out of nowhere, a car ran into the back of my car.

"What the fuck," I shouted. I ran back to the car. The guy in the vehicle got out and took off running. I screamed for people to stop him, but nobody seemed to move or care because people in the hood don't care about shit like that. Jaylen came running over to see if I was okay. I told him I was good, and I called the police.

We waited for about an hour for the police to take the report and tow the other person's car. The officer informed me where to pick up the hit-and-run police report in a couple of days. Then Jaylen and I drove off in my wrecked car. In my mind, I knew Jaylen was going to pay for this shit because I wasn't even supposed to be there.

Still shaken up over the hit-and-run, I decided to skip the strip club. Besides, there were too many cop cars in the parking lot when we passed it. I didn't think it was safe after what I just went through. I had had enough of Zone 3 for the night. Jaylen still wanted to go but agreed to just call in a take-out order from Waffle House. We drove back to his house and spread the food on his coffee table, scarfing down grits, eggs, and chicken melts, while watching reruns of *Martin*.

I'd never spent this much time with Jaylen over the time we'd been knowing each other. It felt kind of weird because I usually just got the money and left. He seemed different tonight. I caught him staring at me several times. It made me feel a little uncomfortable, but I welcomed the distraction to keep my mind off Keith. I felt intrigued to learn more about Jaylen. I never looked at him as nothing more than a trick. Maybe I'd been missing something. He might've been a potential boyfriend after all. I asked him to use his bathroom, so I could freshen up.

After using the bathroom, I snooped through his medicine cabinet. Initially, I found the usual guy stuff: shaving cream, alcohol, and cologne. As I closed it, I spotted a prescription bottle with his name on it. Prozac! I must have shut the mirror hard enough for him to hear.

"You aight in there?" he yelled from the living room.

"Yeah, I'm good. Be right out."

When I opened the door and tip-toed out, Jaylen was right there waiting for me.

"You find what you were lookin' for?"

"What you mean? I wasn't looking for anything but some mouthwash. The onions are on my breath, so I wanted to rinse my mouth out."

I tried to walk off to the living room, but Jaylen yanked me by the hair and threw me into the wall.

"I been tryin' to figure out all night how this shit was goin' to go down."

"Stop, Jaylen! You're hurting me!"

"Bitch, shut the fuck up. You been runnin' round town with my homeboy and thought I didn't know? I should kill yo triflin' ass right here!"

"What are you talking about? *Who* are you talking' about?"

He pushed me to the bedroom. When the door opened, I saw pictures of Keith and me plastered all over the room. Places we'd eaten. Places we'd stayed, and a couple of pictures were taken in front of my house and Keith's loft.

"I bet you know who now, bitch." He pushed my face against one of the pictures, leaned in, and whispered in my ear. "Do he fuck you like JRock?" I felt his gun pressing against my back. I screamed in anguish, begging for my life. The way he was acting, there were only two ways this was going to end; his life or mine.

"Jaylen, please let me explain. It's not what you think."

"Oh, so this ain't you hugged up with my homeboy? I know how my homeboy looks, and I sure as hell know how the fuck yo ass look. You tryin' to tell me this ain't you? Come on, Kim, I know you smarter than that".

"Yes, it's me, but it's not what you think. Please let's sit down and talk about it." He threw me on the bed.

"Talk bitch," he demanded, pointing the gun in my face.

"I know him from selling him clothes. I'm a booster. I never told you about my hustle. Keith and I just meet to make the exchanges. That's it. I didn't know you knew him."

"Kim. Kim. Kim. I know all about you, babe. I know about yo lil hustle. Daisy tells me everything about you." I gave him a shocked look.

"Oh yeeeaah, you didn't know me, and your girl go way back. She's my ride-or-die chick. She's alive because of me, and she will forever owe me." I thought about Daisy and the scars on her body. Did Jaylen do that to her? Oh, my God, what in the world had I gotten myself into?

"What do you want from me, Jaylen? You can have whatever you want. Just let me go."

"Nawl, baby girl, I can't do that. I really had feelings for you, and I thought you felt the same, but you just like the rest. I try givin' you hoes money to ease your life because y'all are always stressin' about bills, bills, and more bills. All y'all be sounding like a broken Destiny Child's record, but y'all don't appreciate me or my efforts. You run to niggas who don't give a fuck about you. You don't think JRock need love too?"

"Jaylen, I think this is a big misunderstanding', love." I tried to sound sincere and unbothered by his bipolar behavior, but I stuttered when I said, "I-I care about you. M-m-more than you know. I want to be with you and only you." I thought I had him convinced, but he looked at me, stroked my face, and tucked my hair behind my ear.

He whispered, "Bitch, if you only wanted me, you wouldn't be fuckin' my homeboy. I can't cross my homie, but if I can't have you, nobody will." He scoffed at me. "Now, take your muthafuckin' clothes off!"

"No, Jaylen, don't do this, please!"

He ripped my blouse, exposing my breasts, ripping my bra off. I begged and pleaded with him, but he ignored me. He paced back and forth, banging on his head with his fist, talking to himself. I stood there, thinking of a plan and searching for something that I could defend myself with, but before I did, he decided to tie me to the bed. He forced my body down and tied my hands to the headboard. I kicked him in the groin. He leaned over, but it didn't faze him. He rose up and laughed.

"Kim, baby, why are you resistin' JRock? I thought you liked bein' with me. When I was payin' yo ass, you were willin' to spread these legs." He took the gun and rubbed it up and down my thigh.

I closed my legs as tight as I could, but he ripped my panties away from under my skirt. He placed the gun between my legs and said, "If you move, bitch I will blow your ass wide open." He unbuttoned his jeans and let his pants fall to the floor. He looked down at my tear-soaked face. "You want JRock, don't you, Kim? You want to cum for JRock, don't you, baby?"

I know he wanted to hear a yes, but I repeatedly said, "No, Jaylen. No!"

"Stop callin' me that! My name is JRock. You should know that by now, stupid bitch!"

He climbed on top of me, prying my legs open, abusing my vagina with his fingers. "Look at my pussy. You been lettin' that nigga fuck you? You let that nigga fuck my pussy, Kim? Why you let him do that, huh? I wasn't giving it to you enough?"

Jaylen appeared to be in his own world. I don't think he even saw me anymore. His eyes were wide and glassy as he continued talking to himself. I didn't know this stranger. In a rage, he raped me as if he had never tried to make love to me. I tried to fight back, but he was too strong. After a few long minutes, I lost consciousness.

When I woke up, Jaylen was sitting on the floor next to the bed, rocking back and forth. He mumbled to himself like a madman. I laid still, trying to make sense of what just happened. I heard Jaylen having a debate with himself.

"I don't want to kill her."

"I have to kill her."

"Yes, she needs to be with the rest of them. She can't be trusted."

"Yes, I love her."

"Yeah, I loved Truffle too, but she betrayed me just like her."

Jaylen contended with his two personalities. To kill or not to kill. I had to find a way to stop him. I began to cry, feeling hopeless, shaking, and trembling. I closed my eyes, hoping to find spiritual strength. There was no sign of God speaking to me like people claimed he did under these circumstances. My mind was spinning. Wait a minute, did he just say Truffle? My eyes popped open.

My voice was raspy from screaming. I whispered, "Jaylen. Jaylen, baby. Please come here. I want to hold you. I know I messed up, baby, but I love you. Can you please forgive me, so we can be together?" I hoped I was talking to the calm personality because I needed to weaken him to make it out of there alive.

"Kim! Are you awake? I'm so sorry, baby. I didn't mean to hurt you. Why you make me hurt you?" he asked.

"It's okay, JRock. But I need you here next to me."

He stood on his knees and shuffled over to the bed. He caressed my face. Without resisting, I leaned my head into the palm of his hand. "I love you, Jaylen," I said as I glanced over at his gun lying on the floor. He crawled beside me, wrapping his arms around me. "Kim, I love you too. Can you please forgive me? I didn't mean to hurt you, baby."

"It's okay, JRock. I understand. I was wrong, and I needed to be punished. It's okay. We'll be okay."

"Yes, Kim. We'll be okay. I'll be better. I promise. I love you more than anything, so I know what I have to do now. Something I should have done a long time ago."

"JRock, can you untie my hands? I want to hug you. I need to hold you, baby."

He thought about it for a second. He contemplated with his inner self whether he should do it or not. He grabbed his gun off the floor and slowly untied me. I gently rubbed both my wrists and reached out to hug him.

"Come on, baby, let Kim hold you." He hesitated but fell into my chest like a child. I sat on the bed, rocking him like a newborn baby. "Tell Kim all about it, baby. Tell me how to love you correctly," I pleaded.

After about two hours of him going on about his life, I learned that Daisy got shot in a robbery gone bad that she and Jaylen set up. They were supposed to run off together with the money and kill Keith and some guy named Trey. I also learned that he was fucking my best friend Tashia at the time she got pregnant. She told him it wasn't his, so he killed her. It had nothing to do with Calvin, as we thought. As much as it hurt me to sit there and listen, I didn't let on that I knew of the people he was talking about. I needed the time to plan an escape. I could hear my phone ringing from the other room.

"JRock, I need to answer the phone. It could be my kids, baby. I don't want them to get worried."

"Aight, I'll go get it for you." He got up with the gun in his hand and went to the living room to get my purse. I had been scanning the room all night for something to use to protect myself. All I saw was a straight razor lying on a plate on the dresser. As soon as he left, I jumped up and got the razor. I slid it under the pillow and sat back in the same spot on the bed.

When Jaylen entered the room, I said, "Thank you so much, baby."

He handed me my purse. I took out my phone as Jaylen stood over me to see who was calling. Thank God I had not programmed Keith's name in my phone under his real name. He was listed in my contacts as Bally. I told Jaylen that it was one of my clients calling about their taxes on the West Coast because of the time difference. I took his hand and pulled him back to the bed. I felt so nasty. We laid on the bed until Jaylen dozed off. He was lying on my arm, so I could barely move. He had the gun in one hand while the other hand was secured around my waist. How the fuck was I going to get out of here? I could feel my eyelids growing heavy from exhaustion. When I opened them, Jaylen moaned and shifted his body but didn't wake up. I looked over at my arm. It was under his armpit, and I could now free it from Jaylen's grip. I reached under the pillow for the razor, and in one sweep, Jaylen's neck was wide open as blood gushed everywhere. He tried to cover it with his hand, but it was too much. He got up, staggering back down to the floor. I sat and watched him continuously trying to inhale. He reached for me a couple of times, but I never budged. Within minutes, Jaylen was gone. I watched all the worthless life drain out of him.

After I collected myself, I walked around the house, opening every closet and dresser, searching for anything that could prove that Jaylen killed Tashia. I found pictures of him and her on her mother's couch in a shoebox in his closet. When I stepped into the closet, the floor squeaked. I remember Jaylen used to stay in the room when I went to wash up after sex. I squatted, unhinging the loose plank. Stacks of money went as deep as I could see, but there was also a small box with a DVD. I scoured the house and found as many bags as I could to pack the money and other contents in. I heard my phone ring. It was Keith. *Baby, I'm so sorry. Please meet me for lunch tomorrow, so we can talk about it, please.*

I began to cry, but composed myself. I didn't have much time, and I needed to get out of here before daylight. I gathered the blood-soiled sheets and put them in a trash bag. Then I took a bleach-soaked sponge and wiped down the areas of where I had been. I also wiped the wall where Jaylen had smashed my face against it. I unplugged the self-surveillance camera wires and made sure it wasn't recording. Once I was done, I pulled Jaylen's body across the hardwood floor, pushed it in the bottom of the closet floor and laid the planks back to normal. I mopped the floor about six times, then broke the mop handle in three pieces, placing all the incriminating evidence, except Jaylen's shirt, in the fireplace and started a fire. It was exhausting but I lugged four bags of money, and camera and recording equipment into the car, keeping note of my surroundings. Finally, I placed the bloody razor blade and the DVD into two separate zip-lock baggies before I left.

During the ride back, memories of Tashia and I came rushing back. She was so young and full of life and that crazy nigga had the audacity to kill her. I slapped the steering wheel in rage. Because of him, the twins grew up without her. Tears began rolling down my face. However, I needed to pull it together. I had work to do, and something told me that the DVD might just be the proof I needed. I headed toward the only person I knew could help.

Chapter Seventeen: Show No Weakness

I pulled into Timothy's driveway at 6:00 am. I hadn't slept in over twenty-four hours. My limbs felt like noodles. I was also in a lot of pain, but I had to push through it. I knew Tim wasn't a morning person, and he hated when people bothered him so early. However, this was an emergency, and I couldn't call before coming. If he hadn't taught me anything else, he taught me to never use a cell phone when doing dirt.

When Timothy opened the door, I fell into his arms.

"Oh, my God! Kim, what happened to you?" Skittish, he looked outside to ensure that there weren't any witnesses watching us or following me.

"Tim, I need your help. Something happened." I handed him the bags with the razor and DVD. Although he saw the blood in it, he didn't hesitate to take it. He placed the bags on the kitchen counter, scooped me up in his arms, and took me upstairs.

"I got you, sweetie. But let's get you cleaned up first. Then you can tell me all about it." I loved that Tim's love or friendship never wavered.

He started the shower and helped me get out of my torn clothes. The hot water felt soothing yet painful at the same time. It felt like tiny needles were pricking each bruise and scrape. I cried out at the slightest touch. I could hear Timothy taking deep breaths as if he was feeling the same pain as me.

When he couldn't take my crying any longer, he stepped in the shower with his clothes on and said, "Let me help you, sweetie. It's okay. I got you." He gently washed my body and calmed my trembling. Tim was truly a good friend. I hated that I had to take him down this dark path with me, but he was the only person I could trust to help. My plan had to be executed in the right way for it to work.

Timothy wrapped my body in one of his bathrobes and guided me to his bedroom sitting area. The warmth of his fireplace relaxed me. I watched the flames of the fire flicker while Tim left the room. A moment later, he came back with chamomile tea, pain medication, and an ice pack. The first sip soothed my soul like the soup my grandmother made whenever I was sick. I filled him in on all the details of Jaylen's psychotic life and how it had intertwined into mine.

"I'm here for you, Kim. Don't worry. We got this. Get some rest, sis. I'll go pick up the kids and take them out for the day".

"Thank you for being so understanding, Tim. I don't know what I would do without you." I climbed into his big king-size bed and drifted off to sleep.

***

I woke up to laughter coming from downstairs. I went to the bathroom first before I had to face whoever Tim invited over. I didn't want them to see me like this. I didn't want them to know the hell I just went through. Although I never had a man flip out on me this badly, in the past, I'd dealt with a few disgruntled sponsors who didn't want to accept a breakup. Jaylen had taken me to a new low. I looked at my face in the mirror. It was bruised and swollen. I stared at myself for a while. It was finally sinking in that I had killed someone. "I killed Jaylen!" I screamed, collapsing to my knees.

"Fuck!" I began hyperventilating as my heart raced. Tim ran in, comforting me.

"Kim. It's okay, sweetheart. I got you. You're safe, baby".

"What have I done, Tim? I'm going to prison! I'm going to lose the twins! They're going to hate me."

"No, they aren't. And no one is going to jail." He reached into the medicine cabinet and grabbed a bottle of aspirin. Turning on the sink, he filled a disposable paper cup with water. "Here, take this." I swallowed the pills and gulped the water down. I was so thirsty and tired, but I needed to calm my nerves.

"That's it, sweetie. We have to get you hydrated and back to your cute self because baby, we got work to do," Tim said with a flip of his wrist.

I knew we had to move on a plan quickly before someone found Jaylen's body. I slowly rose off the floor and took a deep breath.

"You're right. Let me pull it together. Show no weakness."

Tim pushed my hair back behind my ears and lifted my chin with his fingers. I saw the sincerity and security in his eyes.

"That's my girl. The hood is in us, not on us. When you're ready, come downstairs. Someone is waiting for you."

I washed my face, brushed my teeth, and put on one of Timothy's Polo sweatsuits. I checked my phone and saw three texts from Keith. He'd been blowing my phone up since our argument. I must admit, I missed him. Right now, I wished that he was here, but due to the current circumstances of me killing his friend, I didn't know if it was a good idea. Hell, I *knew* that it wasn't a good idea.

Keith: I'm sorry. Can I see you today? We need to talk.

Me: Not today. I'm handling some business with the twins.

I didn't want to lie to him, but if I hadn't learned anything else in these streets, it was that it was never a good idea to set off red flags. For now, I had to make everything seem as normal as possible with Keith.

Keith: OK, hit me up when you free.

Me: Will do.

I walked downstairs and into the living room, not knowing who to expect. To my surprise, it was Tanya. She greeted me with open arms, telling me that everything would be okay and that the twins were with my mom.

"I'm here now, baby girl. We'll get through this," she whispered in my ear.

I was so glad to see her. Tanya and Timothy were the only two people in this world that I trusted. She filled me in on her sobriety and her new man. That's why she had been missing in action for the past few weeks. He seems to be a great guy. It is an unfortunate reunion, and I didn't like the idea of bringing her into my shit, but I needed her help with this, big time.

We sat in the kitchen and started strategizing my freedom. Time was ticking, and Jaylen's body would eventually be found. We needed to come up with something soon, but first things first, we needed to see what was on that DVD.

Chapter Eighteen: The Chase

The last week had been fucked up. I hadn't seen Kim, and I hadn't been able to convince Candi's crazy ass to leave Atlanta. On top of that, JRock still didn't come through to any of the meet-ups with Trey and me. Neither of us hadn't heard from him. I couldn't keep Romero waiting, so I had to put the money up. I knew JRock would hit me back with it later. In the meantime, Trey and I met up with the club owner, Scott, to get our VIP sections for New Year's Eve.

"Man, this shit 'bout to be so lit," I said to Trey as we walked into the building.

"Hell yeah, nigga. This bitch gone be crazy thick," he replied.

"You bringin' yo main girl, right? I need to make sure because I plan on bringin' Kim."

"Yeah, you know she secure all holidays after that shit popped off at that Halloween party we threw at the Flame."

Trey's baby mama popped up on us at the Blue Flame one year. We thought we were throwing a private invite only, *Naked Fright Nite P*arty. She caught Trey in the VIP with his side piece getting sucked and fucked on. Let's just say that was the first time I'd seen that nigga bow down to a female. She beat his ass all the way out of the club in his boxers.

"Who can forget that shit? Nigga, yo ass thought she was gonna kill you when she whipped that gun out."

"Y'all should've been worried too. She thought y'all helped set it up. Shiid, she was ready to bust a cap in y'all ass too."

"Hell yeah. You right." We laughed.

"But man, on a serious note. Have you heard from JRock?"

"Nawl, that nigga ain't hit me back in a few days. Last time I talked to him was the night we went to the strip club. We need to hunt that nigga down in case he in some shit."

"Right, right. I'm goin' by his lil hide-out spot when we leave here and see what I can find out. I'm sure that nigga laid up and trickin' off with some broad."

"Bet. I'll put my ear to these streets and see if anybody heard anything out of the ordinary. You know he be on some wildin' out shit sometimes."

"Facts," I said as we dapped each other. We watched a fine ass chick walk towards us. She looked familiar, but I couldn't place her face.

"Good afternoon, gentlemen. Nice to see you again. My name is Daisy. I'm the club coordinator. I'm glad you've chosen us to help bring in the New Year. I apologize, but Scott is currently in a meeting. So, I'll be taking care of you. You were highly recommended by him. Let me show you what we have planned for you in our VIP section." Daisy led the way to the elevator.

We got off on the second floor. Daisy continued, "This is our luxury all-white VIP room. It comes with a fully stocked bar, two bartenders, two waitresses, a buffet of your choice from our menu, twenty bottles, fifteen of your choice, and five bottles of our best champagne. The room seats up to thirty people, and as you can see, it has a perfect view of the whole club from the glass window. The floor is continuously saturated with smoke to create a luxury fog illusion. The ceiling will be covered with white balloons that will drop at midnight. You'll receive free valet parking for up to thirty cars and a VIP Red Carpet entrance for all guests on your list. So, what do you guys think?"

"We'll take it," Trey and I said in unison.

"Don't you want to know how much it is?" she said with a star-struck expression.

Trey responded with a line from one of our favorite movies, *Shottas*. "If I have to ask the price, that means I can't afford it."

"Okay, then, gentlemen. I'll be right back with the paperwork."

I intervened in this little movie Trey was trying to create. "That's cool and all, baby girl, but you can skip the paperwork. This is a cash transaction, and we don't need no paper trails. If you need to get the owner on the phone to approve it, I'll understand. But can you hurry it up? We got places to be."

"No, I understand. I totally overlooked the notes he left here for me. What name should your guess list have on it?"

"Kash The Don."

"Awesome! The ultimate buffet includes shrimp, assorted wings, a wide variety of finger foods, and our mixed brown and white top-shelf bottle package. That'll be $16,200."

I opened my backpack, counted eighteen bands on the bar, laid Kash's CD on top of the money, and told her to tell the DJ to add it to his playlist.

"It'll be my pleasure. Thank you again for choosing our venue for your New Year's celebration. Let me walk you guys out." When she reached to shake our hand, her red nails and tattoo on her wrist caught my eye.

But before I could entertain my thoughts, Trey said, "Oh, but can I get your number before I go? You know, to go over any questions I may have later?

"Yes. Here's my card. Don't hesitate to call. I'm here to serve," Daisy said.

"Yes, you can definitely serve me," Trey mumbled.

Trey smiled from ear to ear when we walked out into the chilly Atlanta breeze. He was thinking about hitting Shawty's ass, but what I wanted to know was how she knew us. When she introduced herself, she said it was nice to see us *again*. I know this couldn't be the same woman I shot in the bathroom when we robbed, ol' dude. I could've sworn she died. She had to have died, because I shot her. How could she have survived? I needed to find JRock's ass ASAP to fit this puzzle together. After all, he was the one who went back to finish the job.

***

After we left the Velvet Room, Trey and I made our way back to his crib to chill out. We needed to use the downtime to figure out where and why the hell JRock disappeared. I wanted to tell Trey that I knew who Daisy was, but I figured it was best to hold off until I found out the full details of how she fits into our world. If Trey knew the truth, ain't no telling how he might react. I wanted to try and end this year on a positive note. That's why the New Year's Eve party had to be perfect, and it would be as soon as I had my baby walking through those doors with me.

"So, you and Kim good again? You said you bringin' her to the party, so I'm guessin' y'all worked y'all lil shit out, right?" Trey asked, staring out the passenger window.

"Nah, man. We ain't really talked since our argument. I did text her earlier, though. She said that she was busy with her twins today, so I'll hit her up tomorrow."

"The party's tomorrow night, nigga. You need to get on that shit now! You know women need time to get all their shit together before they hit a big scene like this."

"What do you expect me to do? Just drive up to her house with a boom box or some corny shit and confess my love. She's not feeling my ass right now, Bruh. I don't want it to seem like I'm sweating her too hard."

"Nah, nigga. But you do need to let her know how you feel."

"You don't think I've been tryin'? I can't force nobody to do what they don't wanna do. You know that I ain't the bug-a-boo type nigga."

"Maybe that's the problem. Look, bruh, you been my nigga since day one, so I'm gonna keep it one hunnit witcha.

We ain't gettin' no younger. Life is too short to be worried about who dick bigger, you feel me? If you luv that girl, you need to grow a pair of balls and go handle yo business, Nigga. I really am looking at shit differently now man. Real love is rare. I be thinking about how I almost died, after I got shot. Back then, I thought surviving a shooting made me a tough nigga. It wasn't until recently, I figured out the man upstairs had other plans for me. I need to get some shit right, which I'm tryin' to do, startin' with my kids and my ol' lady. That girl has been with me through all my bullshit. It would be selfish for me to leave this world without doing right by her and the kids. If you ain't noticed, I been trying to get my finances together so I can move her and my kids out of the projects. They deserve better. All this money doesn't mean shit if we can't give our kids a better choice than what we had. You wouldn't believe it, but my girl just got her RN certification. She been working on that shit for a minute. I know y'all think she ghetto as fuck, but she straightened that shit up for her career. She's actually smart as hell, which is why we've stayed down so long. I wouldn't leave her for any of these hoes out here in the street. What I'm getting at Bruh, some women need the chase. So, what you gonna do? Keep complaining that your girl won't talk to you or go be about yo business? If you care about her. You need to lock her in and fix all that shit before walkin' into the new year."

Damn. Trey was speaking some real shit right now. I'd never heard this nigga speak facts this deep, but he was right. I needed to get my girl back. I was so serious about Kim that I'd finally told Candi the truth. Well, at least most of it. I told her that I'd fallen in love with someone else and that I didn't feel the same way about her as she did about me. I tried to let her down as gently as possible, but she was still hurt and pissed. I came clean about not being broke too. I just didn't let on exactly how much money I had. I gave her the twenty grands back, and she told me that she wished me the best and that if I changed my mind, she would be there. Honestly, Candi wasn't concerned about taking care of broke niggas. Homegirl needed somebody to love her. She needed real love. Despite adding another fucked up nigga to her roster, I wished her the best. The more time I spent with her over the last couple of days, I realized that she was genuinely a sweet girl. She just had some maturing to do. I know that she would eventually find the right nigga to treat her right.

"You right, Bruh. Lemme go get my girl. Enough of this down and out bull shit," I said.

I dapped Trey up and headed to Kim's house. We were going to hash this out whether she was ready or not. The shit that we were arguing over was so petty. It was time to squash it so we could move forward and be together the way we were meant to be.

***

Ding Dong! I rang Kim's doorbell. After a minute I rang it again. Her car was parked in the driveway, so I knew she was home.

"Can I help you, Hun?" An older white lady said from the slightly opened door.

"Yeah, uh, is Kim here? I need to talk to her. It's important."

"Give me just a minute."

She closed the door in my face. On the other side of the door, I heard Kim's voice in a faint whisper. It sounded like she told the lady to ask me to go away, but that wasn't going to happen. I didn't care how long it took. I wasn't leaving until I got my girl back.

"Kim! Kim! I know you in there. Come on, baby, I just need a few minutes. Please. This shit has been goin' on long enough," I said, talking through the door.

A moment later, the door cracked. Kim peeped through the door.

"What do you want, Keith? I told you I was busy today."

"Yeah, I know, but this can't wait. I have something to tell you."

"Whatever it is, it'll have to wait. I'm not in the mood right now."

"Kim, please. I ain't leavin' until we talk. You know I'm a man of my word."

Kim sucked her teeth and sighed, "Fine. I'm coming out."

A few minutes later, Kim came out dressed in a dark gray sweatsuit. Her face looked like she had gotten into a fight with a mountain lion.

"Wha-what the hell happened to your face? Who the fuck did this shit?" I asked, raising my voice.

"Calm down, Keith. I just got into a car accident, that's all. A hit and run. Some asshole rammed into the back of my car and took off. I'm fine. It's just a few bumps and bruises."

I unclenched my jaw and evened out my breathing. I looked at Kim in her eyes. I couldn't tell if she was telling me the truth, but I chose to believe her at the moment. But if I found out something different, somebody was taking a nap in a coffin.

"Okay. Well, I'm glad you're okay. I miss you, baby. I'm so sorry for gettin' upset at you over this petty shit with Calvin. I should've been more understandin'. I know you've been through a lot, and I have too. I just…I got scared."

"Scared of what?"

"I don't know. I just…I guess I was tryin' to find a flaw in the relationship. What we got is so real, so good, that it felt like it was too good to be true, and when you told me about the twins and Calvin, I used that as an excuse to sabotage us. But I promise I'm done with the bullshit. Just give me, give us a second chance. Please."

"I don't know, Keith. Shit's too complicated between us. Our worlds…they're too small. How can we have a relationship with the kind of life we live? With the people that we know?"

"I don't give a fuck about that or people. Let them do whatever they are going to do. All that matters is us. You mean more than anything to me. I love you, Kim."

"What did you just say?"

I puffed my chest and shouted, "I said, I love you, Kimberly Davison! Life's too short, and I won't spend another moment of it without you."

Kim's eyes grew teary-eyed. She walked closer toward me.

"I love you too, Keith Thomas," she said before kissing me.

I wrapped my arms around her and started kissing the bruises on her face.

"I want to celebrate our getting back together and I want everyone to know you are my girl. I'm hosting a New Year's Eve party at the Velvet Room tomorrow night for my artist. Come with me. It won't feel right bringin' in the new year without you."

Kim let go of my neck and pushed away from me. She fidgeted her thumbs with an uneasy look on her face.

"I'd love to, but I'm really not in the partying mood right now. I've got a lot going on between the twins, work, and dealing with this accident stuff. I just don't think…."

"Whatever it is you got goin' on, I can help you with it. We are a team, babe. It's been a lot for both of us. Let's just enjoy ourselves. I promise you I'll make it worth it. Whatever you need, I got you. I promise." I don't know if I'd convinced her enough or not, but Kim's face lit up like a Christmas tree.

"Okay. I'll go. Why not? We need to have some fun, and it'll be good for us to get back on track. What time should I be ready?" she replied.

"Cool! Be ready by 9 o'clock."

"9 o'clock it is. See you then, Mr. Thomas," she confirmed. Kim kissed my cheek and went back into the house.

Tomorrow night was going to be lit. Between my artist getting signed, getting my girl back, and taking my career to the next level, I'd be starting off the new year strong. The only thing left to straighten out was the chick at the club. I needed answers from her about the day of the robbery. Something didn't feel right about her, and I intended to find out the truth.

Chapter Nineteen: Sorry

I couldn't believe that Keith told me that he loved me. I never imagined that our meeting at a bus stop would turn into this. As happy as I should've felt right now, I couldn't let my guard down too much. When Keith came knocking on my door unannounced, I thought for sure that he figured out that I'd killed Jaylen. The tone in his voice and his persistence made me almost surrender myself. Fortunately, Tanya convinced me to talk to him. She figured that it was better to keep cool. If Keith didn't let on that he knew anything, I wouldn't either.

"Yes, Kim! You look hot, girlie!" Tanya said, snapping her fingers.

"You really think so? These bruises are making me feel so insecure. I don't want Keith seeing these," I lifted my arms, showing Tanya the discoloration that the rope left on my wrists.

I was wearing a black, V-neck, knee-length Armani dress with short-sleeves that I picked up from Neiman Marcus a few weeks ago. I had it on standby for a client, but they decided that they didn't want it. So, I kept it for myself.

"Oh, sweetie." Tanya massaged my wrists. "I'm so sorry this happened to you. I'm sorry I wasn't here when you needed me."

"No, Tanya, it's fine. You were off tryin' to get better, and you have. I'm so proud of you for doin' what you needed to do. We definitely have to throw you an engagement party. I'm so glad you found love. You deserve that and more."

In the weeks that Tanya disappeared, she had checked herself into a rehab facility. She feared that if she didn't seek help, especially after dealing with her family, that she would do something that she regretted. She voluntarily went off the grid, making herself unreachable to focus on herself and stay clean for real this time. She found a great man in the midst of it all. He seems to be a stand-up guy.

"Thanks, Kimmie, but I'm worried about you. If you aren't sure you're ready to get back out there tonight, don't pressure yourself. You, me, and the girls can have our own New Year's Eve Party."

As tempting as Tanya's offer was, I had my own plans outside of being Keith's date to his New Year's Eve party. I didn't want to go with him, but then something dawned on me. Daisy recently started working at the Velvet Room as an event coordinator. I knew that she would most likely be there. Just to confirm, I hit her up and asked her if she had any plans for the night. She told me that she was stuck working at some private New Year's party. Going with Keith was a double win because I would get to bring in the new year with my man and confront this bitch about her betrayal. Jaylen nearly killed my ass because she ran her mouth. She was going to have to answer one way or another for what she did. I didn't want to let Tanya in on my plan because she would've convinced me to take it easy. I didn't have time to sit idle. I needed to put an end to all this shit.

"That's tempting, Tanya, but I'm fine. I promise. I just want to forget about the last couple of days, hell, the last week, and let this man love on me."

"Then have fun, you shall, darlin'. Here! What about this dress instead? It's long sleeve, so it'll cover your wrists," Tanya said as she held up a black Valentino dress with a side-slit.

"I forgot that I had this dress." I hugged Tanya, squeezing her tight.

***

Keith rang the doorbell at 9 pm on the dot. I'd been sitting in the living room with Tanya and the twins for the last half-hour talking. I answered the door.

"Damn! Kim, you...damn!" Keith said, speechless.

"You look good too, babe. Ready?"

"Your chariot awaits, Miss Davison."

"Bye girls. Bye Tanya! I'll be back after midnight. Y'all have fun, but not too much! Muah!" I blew kisses before walking out the door with Keith.

Keith opened my door, helping me slide into the passenger seat. When we got on the road, I asked, "When did you get a new car?"

He smiled, "not too long ago. I was saving it just for tonight. My baby gets only the best."

"You are really working overtime to win me back, huh?"

"I thought I already had you back. You changin' your mind already?" Keith teased.

"No, I'm just saying. Anyway, what have you been up to besides buying cars?"

"Well, I have been doin' somethin'. Check under your seat."

I reached under my seat and pulled a red gift bag out. Pulling the paper out of the bag, I saw a red velvet box.

"Oh my God! Babe! The diamond earrings I saw?" I shouted. Seeing the earrings sitting perched in the box, made me want to cry. I saw them when we went Christmas shopping weeks ago. I didn't know he saw me even looking at them.

Keith smiled and nodded. "I wanted to give it to you the night of...well, you know."

I shook my head. "Thank you, babe. I wasn't expecting anything tonight."

"You deserve it. Besides, seein' you smile and us bein' back together has been the highlight of a really shitty week."

"Why do you say that what happened?"

"Well, besides our fallin' out, my homeboy, Jay, has been off the grid. It ain't like him to be gone this long. If his ass doesn't show up tonight, we know something ain't right so, Trey and I are going to search around for him and see if anybody knows anything."

My throat felt as if it was closing. I gripped the seat. "Oh, really? Well, I'm sure he'll show up soon, babe. Maybe he just got tied up with a female or something." I hoped that Keith hadn't planned to spend most of the evening talking about Jaylen. I was doing the best that I could, remaining as collected and normal as possible.

"Yeah, you're right. But still, I'm going to see what's up. I know he got an uncle that usually hangs around his house. Maybe he'll know something."

"Yeah, that's always a good place to start." My heart was beating out of my chest. "So is your artist getting a lot of traction?" I asked, changing the subject.

"Hell, yeah! He is blowin' up! I played his joint at the strip club the other night, and everybody went wild! It went viral, and I signed him with QC yesterday."

"Strip club?" I said before I knew it. That had to be why Jaylen desperately wanted to go to the strip club that night.

"Uh…yeah. I guess I should tell you that a few of my boys and I hit up the strip club. I uh…"

I grabbed his hand and said, "It's okay, Keith. We were on the outs. Whatever you did during that time is in the past. I don't care about no strip club anyway."

"Yeah, I know. But still, I think you should know that I slept…."

"I don't need to know. We are moving into the new year together, right? Let's just leave it out there. I won't hold anything against you and vice-versa. Cool?"

I sincerely wanted a fresh start with Keith. Whatever he'd done and whoever with, surely couldn't have been worse than what I did to his best friend. Once Tim and I squared away the details around me taking out Jaylen. Hopefully, we wouldn't have to talk about this anymore.

Maybe that made me a little naive, but I had to have some hope, even if it wasn't the most realistic.

"Cool. I needed to hear that, babe. Listen, I don't want us to have any more secrets between us. So, moving forward, I want to be honest with you, and I want you to know that you can trust me with anything too."

"Okay. Sounds good," I said with a faint smile.

***

The party was the most lit celebration I'd been to in a while. I hadn't had any time to party with everything that's been going on, but I wanted to forget about everything for the night and focus on my baby and me and get to Daisy's lying ass. Our section was packed but still pretty quiet. I knew that the other half of the party guests would arrive within the hour, because everyone knows that the party doesn't really start until close to midnight.

"Yo! My nigga! This shit is lit, right?" A big, tall guy said, as he walked up to us. He looked like a mixture of Rick Ross and Biggie, and I could smell the liquor on him before he said a word.

"Yeah, man! Homegirl didn't do this spot justice on that tour. It looks much better at night," Keith replied. I assumed that he was talking about Daisy. He mentioned in the car that he and Trey toured the place ahead of time and that some female helped them out with getting approved without the paperwork. That was the least the bitch could do after attempting to kill them.

"Yo, my bad. This is my girl, Kim. Kim, this is my boy, Trey."

"How are you doin', Kim? It's good to finally put a name to a face. Been hearin' about you for months. Glad Keith finally brought you around us. My girl is on the way. I'll introduce y'all when she gets here," Trey said while throwing back the remainder of his liquor.

"Nice to meet you too. I've heard a lot about you too," I lied. I hadn't heard Trey's name until Jaylen mentioned it that night, but I didn't want to be rude and throw Keith under the bus for not mentioning his friends. Between Jaylen's crazy bipolar ass and meeting Trey, I see why I hadn't met either.

"Damn, nigga, did you drink up all the champagne and shit already? Save some for the guest, greedy ass," Keith said, while he laughed and playfully pushed Trey's shoulder.

I searched the room to see if I could spot Daisy. I knew she would be moving around throughout the night, ensuring that everything was intact with the party. I needed to make my move before the place got too crowded. People loved drama, and if something popped off during my confrontation with Daisy, they wouldn't hesitate to catch the action on Instagram and shit. I didn't have an exact plan on how I wanted to confront Daisy, but I knew that it had to be done sooner than later.

"I'm going to catch up with y'all in a little bit. I'm going to browse around."

"Okay, baby, that's cool. We'll be at the VIP section up here," Keith motioned.

I nodded before taking off. I searched all over for Daisy, she was nowhere in sight. I knew for sure she was here because she told me. She might've been tending to another party or taking care of business in a different room, but I wasn't going to give up until I found her. I clenched my fist, growing agitated by the minute. Keith texted me and asked if I was okay. I assured him that I was fine and that I was going to the bathroom to freshen up. Men understood what it meant for a woman to freshen up. I would be good for at least a half-hour before he checked on me again. Since it was still early, the line for the bathroom was non-existent. I lay my clutch purse on the sink and examined my face. Tanya had helped me cover up the bruise marks on my face and wrists well with foundation. That way, in case Keith wanted to get freaky tonight, I wouldn't have to make up some excuse as to why he couldn't see my body, not that I was in the mood anyway. I'd just been sexually assaulted forty-eight hours ago. Sex was the last thing I had on my mind.

Taking a deep breath and one more glance in the mirror, I adjusted my back length, barreled-curls out of my face, and exited the bathroom. Well, I'll be damned. I stood outside the bathroom and saw Daisy entering another room down the hall with what looked like a bartender. Without hesitation, I followed behind them.

Slam! I shut the door behind me. Daisy and the bartender jumped, startled by the door.

"Kim? Hey, girl, what are you doing here?"

SLAP! Daisy stumbled over a few boxes on the floor. The bartender leaped out of the way as he saw me lunging toward her.

"Bitch! Are you crazy? What the hell you do that for?" Daisy asked, regaining her balance.

"No, bitch, are *you* crazy? How could you betray me like that? You're supposed to be my girl!"

I shot the bartender a *leave us alone* look. He jetted out the door so quickly, I felt the air brush past my legs as he closed the door.

"Wha-what are you talking about?"

"Don't play stupid with me, Daisy. We both know you are not as dumb as you play."

"Kim, I have no idea what you are talking about."

"I know about you and Jaylen, or you might know him as JRock. I know about you and him sneaking behind my back. I mean all of it too, bitch. How you went behind my back and told him about my coming and going. Keeping tabs on me so you could go and report back to him like a lil bitch. Oh yeah, I also know about the robbery. How you two set his boys up to kill them and run off with the money," I fumed.

"Ho-how do you know that? Who told you that? JRock?"

"No. But it doesn't matter who told me or where I got it from. The fact is you lied to me. You betrayed me, and for what? A few dollars? Bitch, if you were in a bind, all you had to do was tell me. I would've done anything for you. We're best friends. At least we *were*."

"Look, it's not what you think, Kim! I-I didn't have a choice! I was…"

"You was what?"

"Look, I had people coming after me. I made a deal with some people a few years back. Shit went left, and I ended up owing people a lot of money. Money that I didn't have. Then I met JRock. He was nice, charming and he knew the game. He knew how to hustle and make shit happen. He told me that if I stuck with him, he would take care of everything for me. That's when he came up with the plan for the robbery. We were going to take all the dude's money and run off together. Nobody was supposed to get hurt. We just wanted a fresh start away from all this shit in Atlanta."

"But why kill Keith and Trey?"

"It wasn't supposed to go down like that, but he knew that if his boys found out what the real plan was, they wouldn't have been willing to help him. We needed the extra set of hands to pull the plan off. They were just a diversion. A distraction, long enough for me to get the money and get out. I was only supposed to be there long enough to get the money and go, but his boys ended up finding me. So, when they saw me, I panicked and shot at them. One of them shot me, and I shot Trey. When they took Trey to the hospital, Jaylen came back for me. He saved me and took me to another hospital."

"So those scars…the scars on your stomach were…"

"From the bullet wounds," Daisy finished my sentence and lowered her head.

I huffed. "So that night that we went to the Drake concert, and you were meeting up with your boo, were you meeting Jaylen?"

"Yeah…"

"And you still let me fuck around with him knowing that y'all had something going on?"

"I knew he wasn't serious about you. You, of all people, should know how these things go. You got to play the game. I knew that when the business was done for the day, he was coming back to me."

"So, you were just going to take off and leave Greg behind? What about your son?"

"I planned to send for him when Jaylen and I were settled. We planned to take Greg out and send Darius with my mom."

"You mean *kill* Greg, right?"

"Yeah."

"That's foul, Daisy. Even for you. I don't like or trust Greg's ass more than the next nigga, but this…all this you are talking about with Jaylen…it wouldn't have worked out the way you think. Besides, Greg is the father of your child."

"Fuck, Greg! He's a womanizing pervert! He was trying to make moves on Candi and thought I didn't know.

He's been doing shit like that for years. I kept overlooking it, praying that he'd change, and he didn't. He's been accused of sexual harassment several times and the radio station kept sweeping it under the rug. Jaylen has been good to me. Better than any nigga in my past. You don't know what me and him got. He could have let me die but he didn't, and that's more than I can say for most niggas."

"I know enough to know that, that nigga ass is crazy!"

"Whatever, Kim. You are just jealous because he didn't fuck with your ass the long way!"

"Wow! Bitch, I could give two fucks about you or him fucking with me," I screamed!

"Yo, what the fuck is goin' on in here?" Keith asked as he burst into the room. I don't know how long he'd been standing behind us, but I hoped that it wasn't long enough to hear Daisy spill the tea on her and Jaylen. His facial expression seemed complex, but he didn't act on anything. I'm assuming he heard nothing.

"Nothing babe. It's just...we are just catching up," I lied.

Keith stared at Daisy and me for a moment. "Well, I got a bartender out there that said somethin' might've been poppin' off back here. Whatever this is, y'all got to wrap this shit up. I don't want the guests riled up over nothing. You good, baby? Do you know this lady or something?"

"Yeah, I'm cool. It's just one of my disgruntled customers. I'll meet you upstairs in a minute. Let me handle this," I insisted.

"Aight, cool," Keith said. He kissed my cheek and slowly left. I could see that he understood this was female business and he need not get involved.

"Why didn't you tell him the truth? You want to, right?" Daisy asked.

"Oh, bitch, you best believe I want to. But I'm not going to."

"Why not?"

"Because unlike you, Daisy, I know how to be fuckin' loyal to the people I care about. If Keith found out the truth about Jaylen, it would break him. I won't do that to him. If he finds out, it won't be from me. But as far as me and you go, we're done. I don't want you calling me, texting me, or nothing. I hope your ass rot in hell. You understand, bitch?"

"Kim, come on, I'm sorry. I didn't mean…."

"Bitch, fuck your sorry. I don't want to hear it. We're done. If I so much as hear a peep about you trying anything against me, Keith, or anyone that we care about, I promise it won't end well for you. I will blow your whole life up and you know I can and will".

Daisy nodded as fear crept on her face. I knew that she would try to do something anyway, but once she found out that Jaylen was dead, she would lose any leverage that she had. I wanted to feel bad for her because I knew she cared for him, but any sympathy that I would've had was gone now. I gave Daisy another piercing look before collecting myself, leaving her in the small room.

Chapter Twenty: Close Call

Daisy had been calling my phone non-stop since Keith's party. I couldn't believe that she and this nigga had been playing on my intelligence for the past couple of years. Shit hurts like a muthafucka. I knew she was blowing my line up to find out where Jaylen was. Fuck, he'd probably told her he was with me that night, but I couldn't worry about her Judas ass right now. I knew Daisy. Eventually, she would dig her own grave and bury herself in it. Karma was a bitch, and I knew that it would bite her sooner or later. The old me would've taken her ass out myself or found someone else to do it. Instead, I'd let fate decide what to do with her, because what she didn't know was that Jaylen had her ass on tape as well.

I'd been thinking about all the times Jaylen was spying on me without me knowing it. It haunted me, knowing that he was lurking around Keith and the twins. I didn't understand why he was so upset with us. Especially if he was in love, the way Daisy claimed they were. I planned on finding out the whole truth, but first, I needed to kill two birds with one stone. Getting Calvin out of jail with the information Tim and I recovered on the tape and disposing of Jaylen's body.

Timothy said that he needed to have the DVD authenticated and sent to the District Attorney anonymously, which was where Tanya came in. No one took a second look when she bumped into the delivery guy outside the DA's office, letting the copy of the DVD fall to the floor with his other packages. We just needed to wait for a call from the DA with a deal to release Calvin.

In the meantime, we needed to get rid of Jaylen's body.

"Okay, ready?" Tim asked.

Tim, Tanya, and I were sitting outside of Jaylen's house, preparing ourselves to do the deed.

"Not, really, but we got to do it. Once this shit is done, we can move on," I said, biting my nails.

I'd been in the streets a long time and had seen and done certain things that the average person wouldn't have been able to do, but this had me scared shitless. If it weren't for Jaylen's ties to Keith, I probably wouldn't have felt as guilty, but Jaylen was his childhood best friend. I knew Keith was understanding of a lot of things, but I couldn't see how he'd understand this one. We'd already been through so much. If his reaction to me telling him about Jaylen didn't go correctly, I could lose him forever. Therefore, getting rid of Jaylen was the safest choice. So, Tim, Tanya and I made a pact that once we took care of this, we'd never speak of it again. As much as Tanya babbled, I knew this was one secret that even she *could* keep.

"We got your back, baby girl," Tanya said, patting my back.

I sighed. "Okay. Let's go."

We hopped out of the throwaway car Tim got from one of his homeboys that owned a junkyard. We couldn't risk being seen in either of our vehicles in case someone showed up. Jaylen's uncle had been out of town for the last couple of weeks, so, fortunately, he hadn't been there to check on things. I picked the lock to the side door.

"Alright, Tanya, you remember what to do. Stay here and keep a lookout. If you see somebody, give the signal. Remember, to tap on the trash can three times."

"Three times. Got it." She repeated.

"Alright. Come on, Tim, let's go."

Tim and I made our way inside and went to the closet. I attempted to pull the floorboards up.

"Damn!"

"What's wrong?" Tim asked, holding the flashlight in my direction.

"The floorboards. I think they're jammed."

"Here, let me try." Tim gave me the flashlight and attempted to pull the floor up.

"Got it! That damn thing didn't want to give. I don't know how you got this thing opened the first time, girl." "Guess I got lucky," I shrugged.

We pulled the rest of the planks up, uncovering Jaylen's body. Immediately the smell of decomposed flesh hit us, and we pulled up our masks over our faces to conceal the smell of his decomposing body.

"Okay. You step back, and I'll pull him out," Tim said.

I was grateful to have him and Tanya there with me to help me out. I couldn't imagine doing all this alone. I was still traumatized just being in this house.

"Oh, God!" I said, holding my stomach.

"You okay, sis?" Tim asked.

"Yeah. Just a little nauseous. I think it's just the smell seeping through the mask. I'm fine. Let's just hurry up." Tim began dragging Jaylen's body out onto the floor.

Click! "Don't move. Hands up," a deep, male voice said behind me. I felt cold metal pressed against the back of my head and I calmly put my hands up. He ordered Tim to do the same.

"Turn around," the man demanded.

We turned around with our hands still up. Once we were facing him, I saw him holding Tanya, gripping her neck with his thick arm.

It was dark in the house, but I could make out his face with the flashlight's faint luminance. It was Jaylen's uncle, Cliff.

"Cliff?" I said, squinting.

"Quiet! Now, I don't want to have to hurt anybody tonight, but I need to know what the hell is goin' on in here. Ain't no sense in lyin'. So don't even try it."

"Fine. I'll explain," I gulped. "Just please…don't hurt Tanya, please."

"I won't have to if you tell me what I need to know."

"Alright. Jaylen…he's…he's dead."

"Well, that's obvious, sweetheart. What I need to know is why and how?"

"I-I…I killed him because…he attacked me! He hit me, tied me up, and raped me! The muthafucka tried to kill me! I had to defend myself."

Cliff stood silent for a moment. He let Tanya go and walked away. I went to hug her, ensuring her that she would be okay. Cliff flipped the lights on and took a seat on the couch. He sat the gun down next to him and massaged his temples. He shook his head and took a few deep exhales. My chest grew heavy watching him. I wasn't sure what he was thinking or what he planned to do. I hoped that we would be leaving out of there alive.

Cliff took one more exhale and said, "Thank God. The muthafucka is finally dead."

Tim, Tanya, and I looked at each other confused.

"I'm sorry…did you just say…thank God? As in…are you actually happy?"

Cliff let out a light chuckle. "Yes."

"Okay, I think you need to explain," I said, eyebrow raised.

Cliff lifted his head and looked at me. "I'd been tryin' to kill that evil bastard for a while now. That's why I've been livin' here. I was substituting his meds with them fentanyl pills hoping he would overdose, but his ass wasn't taking them".

"What? Why?" I asked, astounded.

"He killed my wife."

"Wait. What? How do you know?" Tim asked

"Well, I didn't know at first. I suspected it though. He and his mother had been at odds for years. About six months ago, when she passed, Jaylen argued with my wife, Shelia, over who would get his mother's inheritance. His mom had a quarter of a million dollars saved. She'd planned to do a will and leave everything to Shelia, but she died before that could happen. We all knew that she didn't want Jaylen to have the money. So, Shelia petitioned the court for help. He killed her before anything could be done". Cliff sniffed, holding back tears. "Jaylen been trouble since he was a kid. It just got worse as he got older. Sheila told me that she was goin' to meet Jaylen somewhere to come to some type of agreement over the money, but she never came home. I called Jaylen, but he would never answer my calls. I even came over here, but he wasn't home. He disappeared somewhere for a few days."

"Did you file a missing person's report?" Tim asked.

"Yeah, they looked into it for a week before they gave up. They interrogated Jaylen, but miraculously, he had an alibi to cover him for the night she went missin'. After that, I didn't want to fool around with the cops. Pigs don't give a fuck about us niggas in the hood, no way. I told him I had nothing left and needed a place to stay. His evil ass wanted me around to gloat, I guess."

"Oh my God," I said, shaking my head. "I'm sorry, Cliff."

"Not as sorry as I am. But you doin' what you did...well...that might've just been a sign from God. I didn't want to kill him, but he surely needed to die. If there is a devil, he was the closest thing to it," Cliff said.

Knock, Knock, Knock! "Yo, Jay! You in there, Bruh?"

I heard Keith's voice on the other side of the door. "Shit! What the hell is he doing here?" I whispered to no one in particular.

"Open up, nigga! We know you here!" Trey yelled out.

Keith and I were supposed to be together tonight for a date, but I changed my plans and told him that I had a girl's night in with Tanya and the twins. He told me that he was going to take care of some business out of town, but I didn't expect his business to be at Jaylen's house.

"Fuck! What are we going to do? Keith can't know that I'm here."

"Don't worry. I'll take care of it. You all just stay quiet," Cliff said, walking to the door.

Cliff cracked the door open and talked to Keith. I heard Trey's voice mumbling something.

"I'm sorry, gentleman, he's not here."

"Where he at? His car here?"

"Uh…I don't know, actually. I just got back in town earlier today. I haven't been able to reach him." Cliff maintained the cracked door.

"Well, that's actually why we are here. We haven't heard from him, either. We tryin' to make sure ain't nothin' happen to him."

"Oh well, I'm sure he's alright. You know how he is. Boy can never seem to stay in one place too long. Listen, when he comes back, or I hear from him, I'll let him know you fellas stopped by."

"Aight…cool. We'll catch you later, Cliff."

"Y'all fellas be cool," Cliff said, closing the door.

"Shit! That was close. I thought for sure he was going to find out," I said. I wasn't sure if he and Trey believed Cliff or not. Between our raggedy hooptie in the driveway and Cliff's covertness, they might still be lurking around, but I did know that we needed to finish the job before they decided to come back.

"Listen, I know why y'all came back. You need to get rid of Jaylen's body. It seems that you've already been through enough. I'll take care of it for you."

"Cliff we…I can't let you do that."

"Yeah, we can't. Besides, how do we know that we can trust you? How do we know you're not lyin'?" Tanya asked. "Listen, I know for a fact that my wife was killed by my nephew. No one wanted him gone more than me. So do you want my help or not?"

I looked at Tim to see what he thought. With a hopeful look, he nodded and said, "Okay. Let him do it."

"Okay. Thank you, Cliff. I don't know how to repay you," I said.

"You don't have to thank me. Just keep quiet and stay the hell away from here, and we'll call it even. I'm just sorry that this happened to you. But at least the muthafucka can't do this to anybody else. Now go ahead, get out of here. I got this."

"Say no more. Come on, y'all, let's go," Tim said.

Before we left, I asked Cliff, "Hey, Cliff. You never told us how you found proof that Jaylen killed your wife. How did you find out?"

"Once I started living here, it didn't take long to find evidence. The sick fucker kept a set of DVDs in the attic confessing to every murder he committed along with a trophy from each victim. Shelia's watch was among them. I sent it to the police, and they haven't done anything about it."

My blood ran cold. I couldn't believe it. Jaylen was actually a certified serial killer. I'd been sleeping with a straight up killer, and I didn't know it. Tim, Tanya, Cliff, and I agreed that we would never speak about this night to each other or anyone again, but justice for what Jaylen had done to Truffles and every other woman would see the light of day, even if he didn't suffer for it. We would make sure that these women knew that someone cared about their story.

Chapter Twenty-one: The Calm Before the Storm

18 Months Later

"Da-da!" My son, Michael, yelled, running toward me.

"Hey, little man! You havin' fun so far?"

"Yesh!" He replied in his baby voice.

I picked him up and gave him a massive kiss on the cheek.

"Hey, baby," Kim said, following him out of the house. "Don't let those links burn. I don't want you burning down my house," she teased.

"You mean our house?" I asked but correcting her.

"Yes. Our house. Don't burn our house down trying to show out for these folks. Remember, I'm the better cook, anyway."

"Yeah, yeah, whatever. You just go and enjoy yourself. Leave your man to this. I got you," I winked, slapping her behind. Kim rolled her eyes, smiled, and ignored my male ego.

"Come on, baby. Let's go play in the bouncy house," she said as she grabbed Michael from my arms. They ran off to play in the yard with the rest of the kids.

A few weeks after we got back together, Kim told me that she was pregnant. Although we knew there was a likely chance that she was pregnant, neither of us was sure that we were ready to bring a baby into the world, but we were confident in each other and knew we could do it. Seven months later, Michael Landon Thomas was born. We named him after our favorite MJs, Jackson, and Jordan.

Shortly after Michael's birth, Kim and I decided it would be best to live under the same roof. Since her house had more space, I moved in with her. I didn't want to get rid of my place just yet, so I rented it out as an Airbnb for a legit cash flow.

Today, we were throwing a barbecue to celebrate our baby boy's first birthday. We were also celebrating Kim opening her own tax company. I was proud to celebrate both my babies. The bonus was that we got to celebrate with our family. Kim's mom, Lisa, and her brother, Derek, came up from their hometown. Even my mom and my daughter came. I was glad to finally reach an agreement with my baby mama to allow Ariel to stay with us during the summer. That way, she could spend time with the twins and her brother. Even Mr. Shepard, my old Principal and Tanya came by. I can't believe Tanya was his significant other. Man, it's a small world.

"Yo, Keith Sweat! What up, man?" Calvin said.

"Yo, Cal! What's good, my dude? How you feelin' out here in these Atlanta streets?" I asked, giving him dap with my free hand.

"Feelin' like a free man!"

"I hear that, my nigga! I hear that."

"Mmmm! Those links sure do smell good. I can't wait to get a couple."

"They'll be ready soon, my boy. How's the new job been treatin' you?" I handed Calvin a beer out of the cooler.

"It's goin', man. It ain't the money I'm used to seein', but it's betta than bein' where I been for the decade and a half. Still, anything is better than hustlin' back out on these streets. I can't afford to go back to jail and be away from my kids again, man."

"I feel you. I'm tryin' to ease myself out of the game too. I never thought I would, but now I have a family. Kim and the kids, man, they are my world, Bruh. Plus, I gotta be an example to my lil man."

"True, true. I appreciate all you and Kim are doing for mine, Bruh. For real, I couldn't have ever imagined this. God sure has a sense of humor. Aye yo, you still ain't heard nothin' bout ya boy?" Calvin asked.

"JRock? Nawl, man. They still got the case open as a missin' person. After puttin' up posters and interrogating' niggas three times over, we hit a dead end. The only person that might know anything is his uncle, but that nigga left town months ago. Ain't nobody seen or heard from his ass since. His sister told us some detectives have been by her house a couple of times looking for Jay. The way she described them; it sounds like the FEDs. So, I'm not sure what the fuck is going on. It's fucked up because we can't be on it like we need to be if them folks lookin' for him too. You feel me? We just gotta lay low and keep our eyes and ears open. Hell, Jay and his uncle might be together for all we know. Come to think of it, when me and Trey went by Jay's spot a while ago, Unc was acting kinda shaky. I hope he wasn't trying to give us a sign or something and our ass missed it."

"Damn, Bruh. That's a hard pill to swallow, man. I'm sorry to hear that. These streets can be hell, but you're right, if the FEDs are looking for him for some shit, you don't want to be anywhere near his fuck ups. Them people work off evidence and that's all they do is try to put two and two together."

"Right, Bruh, but it's all good. It is what it is. I'm hoping he turns up soon dead or alive. You feel me?" I took a sip of my beer as I flipped the links and burgers over on the grill.

"Well, I hope you get the word you need, dawg. I know all too well how it feels to lose a homie and a loved one."

"Thanks, man, I appreciate it."

I wasn't convinced that JRock was alive, but I wanted to know what happened and why it happened. I knew Jay was impulsive, hot-headed, and ruthless at times, but he was still my best friend, and no matter what, he would always be. If I find out who did this, they will have to stand on it or die on it.

"Hey, Keith!" Candi greeted me as she strutted up the driveway and interrupted our conversation.

"Hey, Candi. How are you doin'?"

"Good, can't complain. I got a gift for Michael and Kim. Where should I put it?"

"Oh, you can put it inside on the living room table with the rest of the gifts."

"Cool. Where's Kim?"

"She is out there near the bounce house with the kids in the backyard and the rest of the family. You can go ahead. Most of the food is ready and on the table. You can grab a plate and help yourself."

"Okay. Thanks!" Candi walked away as Calvin eyed her from behind.

"Yo, who was that?"

I said, "She's an old friend. She's a mutual friend of Kim and me. Why, you tryin' to holla?"

"Hell, yeah! She fine, fine! You gonna hook ya boy up?"

I laughed and said, "Yeah, man. I got you. But I should tell you, we got history."

"Shiid, it's all good. We all leftovers to somebody. I'm just trying to hit something, Bruh. Plus, I know you got Kim. You ain't checkin' for no more hoes in these streets."

"Hell, yeah. You right, I ain't. That shit dead."

Life has truly been crazy this past year. I finally got around to asking Kim about her little encounter with that chick at the New Year's Eve party. She told me that she and Daisy were close, but when she tried to confront her about stepping out on her husband, Daisy got offended and came after Kim. Later, I found out that Candi and Daisy were cousins after Kim invited Candi over for dinner. At the same time, Candi realized that the girl I left her for was Kim. That shit was tense as hell, but to avoid any awkwardness, I came clean and told Kim about my history with Candi. She didn't care, though. She understood street business, and she trusted me enough to know I wouldn't do anything to hurt her. She's right, and for that, I'll always be truthful to her. As far as Kim and Candi went, I guess none of that mattered. Ever since they both kicked Daisy's ass to the curb, they have been like two peas in a pod. After Kim broke ties with Daisy, I could see how much it hurt her. With that said, I decided not to confront Daisy about that day of the robbery, until I found JRock's ass. She would get hers when the time was right. Candi and I kept things respectful and cordial between us. I had been hoping that she would find a dude who would be down for her. Looks like Calvin wanted to be that nigga.

"Come on, baby! We are about to cut the cake soon," Kim called out to me.

"Aight, here we come, babe! I'm just takin' off the last of the meat."

I stared at my girl as if I'd just met her for the first time. She was so beautiful. She was glowing with happiness. I swear, Kim made me the happiest man in the world, and I wanted to spend the rest of my life with her. Still, I didn't know if I would ever be able to tell her that I was there when both Daisy and Truffles got shot.

***

"Hey Kim," Calvin said, walking toward me with a full plate of food.

"Hey, Cal. You enjoying yourself, Big Brother?"

"Yeah, sis. Enjoyin' being' a free man. I can't thank you enough for doin' what you did." I don't know how you and Tim did that shit but I'm forever grateful.

"I told you, you don't have to thank me, Cal. We are family. It's what we do. Besides, you know you would've done the same."

After two weeks of impatiently waiting on the DA to review the DVD of Jaylen confessing to killing Truffles, the court pushed for Calvin's release from prison, but it still took another few weeks for his release to go through the proper channels. They had to ensure that they had enough evidence that Jaylen really committed the crime. I bet if it was a white man, they would've released him the same day. Thankfully, Cliff had sent the other evidence in anonymously. A pattern like that was grounds for a serial killer profile. So, the FBI was all over it. I didn't tell Calvin the whole truth about Jaylen, but I let him know enough so that he would be satisfied. I don't think Tim told him much on the legal end either. Other than knowing Jaylen's government name, there was no need to discuss it any further. Calvin didn't want to know, anyhow. He was just glad to be out of that hell hole and be back with his daughters.

"You ready for some cake? Or are you still stuffing your face with ribs," I asked, laughing at Calvin scarfing down his food. God knows he hadn't had a decent meal since being locked up. It was good to see him enjoy himself.

"Yeah, I'm good, sis. Go ahead. I'm still programmed to watch the news at this time of day. Do you mind if I turn the TV on?"

"Of course not. The remote over there on the coffee table."

I gathered my family around the patio table holding Michael's birthday cake. Keith was also sweet enough to get some cupcakes to celebrate my opening the tax office.

"Okay, everybody. First, I just want to thank y'all for coming out and celebrating Michael's birthday and my new business."

"Of course! Where else would we be," my mom shouted.

"You deserve it, Kim," Tim said, pumping his fist.

"Thanks, y'all. I wouldn't have made it without all of your support. Keith and I have reached so many milestones in such a short period of time. We've moved in together, we have a beautiful son, a blended family, a new business, and the girls got their dad back. My heart is full," I said, growing misty-eyed.

"All I can say is thank you, thank you, thank you! Now, who's ready to sing happy birthday to the birthday boy," I said, placing Michael on the picnic bench in front of his cake.

"Wait a minute, babe. Before we do that, I have somethin' I want to say." Keith said, taking my hand.

My heart leaped as he grasped both hands, staring me in the eye. "Kim, from the moment I met you, from the minute I saw you, I knew you were somethin' special. I knew when I asked you out to lunch that I would get to experience that specialness. I know we've been through many tests and trials, but I'd like to think that we passed them all. I think as long as we're together, we can pass the others down the line. I love you. I love our family more than anything in this world. I want to be with you every day for the rest of my life," Keith said while kneeling on his right knee, holding onto my left hand.

"Kimberly Lynn Davison, will you marry me?"

I gasped, clutching my chest. My family shouted out their yes before I could get the word to come out of my mouth. "YES! YES, I'll marry you, baby! Oh, my God!"

Our family cheered us on, taking pictures and posting them to Instagram, Facebook, and wherever else they could. I wrapped my arms around Keith and kissed him. We whispered "I love you" in each other's ear, taking in the moment. As I stared into Keith's eyes, I knew that we would have a lifetime of blissfulness, but subconsciously, the night with Jaylen still haunted my mind. I didn't know if I could ever tell Keith that I killed his best friend.

At that very moment, Calvin loudly called me and Tim's name and said, "Y'all need to come and see this." Everyone turned to see the seriousness in Calvin's face. Keith, Tim, and I went to the living room.

There was a Breaking News Report of two serial killers on the TV screen. Jaylen and Daisy's pictures were plastered all over the screen. We all stood there staring at the screen, speechless, while the news reporter spoke, *"A long and exhausting search has ended for Jaylen Allen, a serial killer with murders dating back several years. His body was reportedly found in the trunk of his girlfriend's car. Daisy Jones, wife of well-known Radio personality Greg "Beat" Jones, was arrested without incident. Mrs. Jones is being held at the Fulton County Jail for murder of Allen and a list of other charges. More on this story tonight at 11. In other news, two Fulton County School teachers have tested positive for Coronavirus. Superintendent Mike Looney is scheduled to announce school closings in a press conference later today. President Trump has stated that the United States is in the preliminary stages of a Pandemic."*

"This muthafucka killed my baby mama and tried to ruin my life. Now, look how his ass ended up, Fuck Nigga shoulda been dead." Calvin shouted.

"What the fuck? Cal, that's my boy, whatcha mean he killed your baby mama? Kim what the fuck going on baby? Did you know your girl had some shit to do with my boy being missing? She killed my boy."

I couldn't answer him. I thought I was going to pass out. Keith held my hand so tight hoping for a response before his phone started to ring. He let go and I flopped down on the sofa with Michael in my arms. It seemed like everyone was on their phone. Candi was shouting in her phone to her mom. Tim was hollering into his about legalities with his office assistant. I sat there in a daze. The room was spinning. Today was the calm before the storm. Daisy is sitting in jail with my life in her hands. She has enough information on me and Keith to put us both away forever. There's no way I can let her, or Jaylen take me from my son. I sat Michael down on the sofa and stood up.

"Everybody except, Tim, Cal, Tanya, Candi, and Keith get the fuck out!' I shouted.

"Kim baby, I'm your mother ..." My mother started.

"I love you, mama. Please take all the children to your house. I'll call you later but right now, I need to handle something."

After everyone was gone, I stood in the middle of the room to address the people I had summoned. "Y'all are my family and I hope after I say what I have to say, we will still be family. First, let's address the elephant in the room. We are all connected to this bullshit with Daisy and Jaylen in some way or another, whether we understand it or not. We all are probably on a person of interest list. Therefore, today we are going to lay all this shit on the table so we can fix it. Tim, correct me if I'm wrong, if we each pay you some money for a retainer, we are covered under Attorney-Client privilege?"

"Yes," Tim replied.

I went to my purse and handed him five dollars. "Here, this should cover everybody." Everybody looked at each other not knowing each other's secrets but knowing we had no choice but to trust each other.

"Are we all in?"

"We in." Everyone said in unison.

"Good. I'll go first, Jaylen and I..."

To Be Continued in the Hood Pandemic...

Made in the USA
Columbia, SC
16 May 2022

60482744R00128